ALL GIRL 5

LESBIAN EROTICA BUNDLE

EROTICA THEMED BUNDLES
BOOK 17

VICTORIA RUSH

VOLUME 7

EROTICA THEMED BUNDLES - BOOK 17

COPYRIGHT

ALSO BY VICTORIA RUSH

Adult Fairytales:

The Enchanted Forest: An Erotic Fairytale

The Land of Giants: An Erotic Fairytale

The Dragon's Lair: An Erotic Fairytale

Witch's Brew: An Erotic Fairytale

The Mage's Spell: An Erotic Fairytale

The Mermaid Lagoon: An Erotic Fairytale

The Coven: An Erotic Fairytale

Rapunzel: An Erotic Fairytale

The Seven Dwarfs: An Erotic Fairytale

The Land of Mutants: An Erotic Fairytale

The Erotic Temple: A Sexy Fairytale (Coming Soon)

Erotica Themed Bundles:

Voyeur: Lesbian Erotica Bundle

Public Affairs: A Lesbian Anthology

Futa Fantasies: The Ladyboy Collection

Threesomes: The Lesbian Collection

Threesomes - Volume 2: The Lesbian Collection

First Time: A Lesbian Anthology

Hedonism: An Erotic Anthology

Switch Hitters: Bisexual Erotica

Taboo Erotica: The Lesbian Series

BDSM: The Lesbian Collection

Party Games: The Erotic Collection

Party Games 2: The Erotic Collection

All Girl 1: Lesbian Erotica Bundle

All Girl 2: Lesbian Erotica Bundle

All Girl 3: Lesbian Erotica Bundle

All Girl 4: Lesbian Erotica Bundle

Erotic Fairytale Bundles:

Clover's Fantasy Adventures: Books 1 - 5

Clover's Fantasy Adventures: Books 6 - 10

Erotic Fantasy:

Pirate's Bounty: A Time Travel Adventure

Wild West: A Time Travel Adventure

Private Riley: A Time Travel Adventure

Cleopatra's Secret: A Time Travel Adventure

Bounty Hunter 2125: A Time Travel Adventure

Ninja Assassin: A Time Travel Adventure

The 300: A Time Travel Adventure

Arabian Nights: An Erotic Fairytale (coming soon...)

Steamy Time Travel Bundles:

Riley's Time Travel Adventures: Books 1 - 5

Lesbian Erotica:

The Dinner Party: Lesbian Voyeur Erotica

The Darkroom: Bisexual Voyeur Erotica

Naked Yoga: Lesbian Transgender Erotica

Nude Cruise: Bisexual Voyeur Erotica

Rush Hour: Taboo Public Sex

The Girl Next Door: First Time Lesbian Erotic Romance

Girls' Camp: Lesbian Group Sex

Wet Dream: Ladyboy Fantasy Erotica

The Convent: Taboo Sex with a Nun

Sex Robot: A Dream Sex Machine

The Personal Trainer: Getting Pumped at the Gym

The Dominatrix: BDSM Lesbian Domination

Webcam Chat: Lesbian Online Sex

Paint Me: A Kinky Bodypainting Workshop

The Toy Party: Girls Sharing Sex Toys

The Costume Party: Strapping One On

Swedish Sauna: Lesbian Group Sex

The Therapist: Taboo Lesbian Erotica

Elevator Shaft: Bisexual Threesomes Erotica

Ladyboy: Lesbian Transgender Erotica

Peep Show: Lesbian Voyeur Erotica

The Dare: Public Sex Erotica

Maid Service: Lesbian Threesomes Erotica

The Hitchhiker: First Time Lesbian Erotica

The Housesitter: Spycam Lesbian Erotica

The Spa: Lesbian Group Orgy

Parlor Games: Blindfold Sex Party

The Exchange Student: First Time Lesbian Erotica

The Hostel: Bisexual Group Erotica

The Harem: Lesbian Erotic Romance

The Orient Express: Lesbian Voyeur Erotica

The First Lady: A Forbidden Lesbian Erotic Romance

The Slave: Lesbian BDSM Erotica

The Masseuse: Lesbian Sensuous Erotica

Too Close for Comfort: Lesbian Forbidden Erotica

Naked Twister: A Wild Party Game

Lexi: The Sex App (Lesbian Fantasy Erotica)

Call Girl: Lesbian Bisexual Threesomes Erotica

Circle Jill: Lesbian Masturbation Workshop

The Viewing Room: Masturbation Voyeur Erotica

Spin the Bottle: A Kinky Party Game

The Hair Salon: Lesbian Voyeur Erotica

Tribadism 1: Girls Only Sex Workshop

Tribadism 2: The Art of Scissoring

Tribadism 3: Threeway Hookups

The Kiss: A Game of Oral Sex

Pledge Week: Sorority Sisters

Carny Games 1: A Wild Sex Party

Carny Games 2: A Kinky Sex Party

Carny Games 3: An Erotic Sex Party

Dreamscape: An Artificial Reality Game

Glory Hole: Guess Who's On the Other Side

Joy Ride: A Late Night Erotic Bus Trip

The Blind Girl: An Erotic Romance(Coming Soon)

Lesbian Erotica Bundles:

Jade's Erotic Adventures: Books 1 - 5

Jade's Erotic Adventures: Books 6 - 10

Jade's Erotic Adventures: Books 11 - 15

Jade's Erotic Adventures: Books 16 - 20

Jade's Erotic Adventures: Books 21 - 25

Jade's Erotic Adventures: Books 26 - 30

Jade's Erotic Adventures: Books 31 - 35

Jade's Erotic Adventures: Books 36 - 40

Jade's Erotic Adventures: Books 41 - 45

Jade's Erotic Adventures: Books 46 - 50

Fifty Shades of Jade: Superbundle

Standalone Stories:

The Polynesian Girl: A Lesbian EroticRomance

For the uninhibited...

WANT TO AMP UP YOUR SEX LIFE?

Sign up for my newsletter to receive more free books and other steamy stuff. Discover a hundred different ways to wet your whistle!

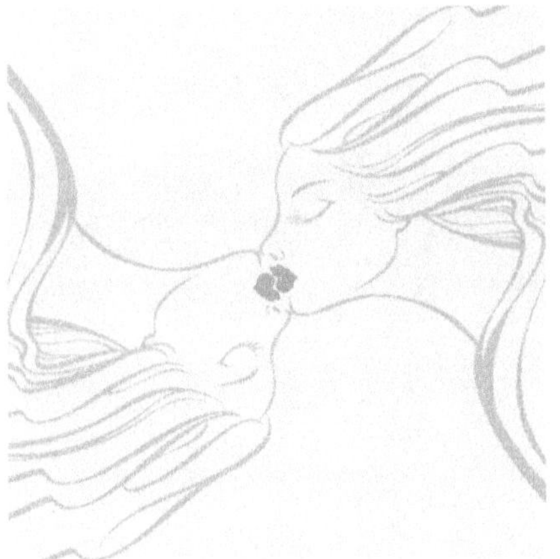

Victoria Rush Erotica

THE MASSEUSE

AN EROTIC ADVENTURE

1

———

Ever since my playdate with Hannah at the rooftop spa in downtown Chicago, I felt a certain void in my love life. I'd enjoyed the various flings with my many lovers over the past few months, but there was always an expectation when the sex was over to move on to the next stage of intimacy. If either partner wasn't ready to invest further in the relationship, inevitably someone's feelings got hurt when one or the other walked away. Every now and then, it was nice to just have a simple, no-strings-attached, take-no-prisoners *hook-up*.

But it was more than that. I longed for the experience of being *feted*, of having my body worshipped by someone whose only focus was giving me the maximum amount of pleasure in the limited amount of time we were together. I wanted to return full-circle to my first experimental foray into the world of anonymous sex at the Fantasy Feast dinner party where I could lie back and let someone service my body. Even if I had to pay for it.

One lonely night when I needed to feel the touch of someone's else's hands on my body, I flipped open my laptop and typed in the search words *private masseuse*. I knew it had to be a female, not a man. Beyond my rapidly increasing proclivity toward having sex only with other women, the kind of massage I had in mind involved more than just the typical therapeutic rub-down. When things got hot and heavy, I needed my partner to keep his dick in his pants while focusing his attention only on pleasing me.

Which was something I'd found very few men capable of doing.

The first few results that came up on the screen provided a list of 'licensed massage therapists' who were available to make house calls in my area. But I knew this was code for the traditional, non-sexual type of massage. Besides, I wasn't sure I wanted my new paramour to know where I lived. Beyond the prying eyes of my nosy neighbors, I didn't want to experience another awkward moment when I had to kick another putative lover out of my house. I wanted to walk in, an out, freely on my own terms from this professional relationship.

I scrolled a little further down the page and hesitated when I saw a listing titled *White Orchid Massage—experience the pleasure of tantric massage.*

Okay, I thought. This sounds a little bit more like what I'm looking for. The word 'tantric' suggested a slightly *different* kind of massage treatment.

I clicked on the link and a description appeared beside a picture of a scantily clad masseuse massaging a woman's bare lower back:

Tantric massage is the art of caressing one's body where the boundaries disappear and the recipient learns to experience an elevated and prolonged form of pleasure and relaxation. Your energy flow is stimulated by our personal Goddesses while your senses are gradually awakened toward their maximum potential. Particular attention is focused on attending to the sensitive personal areas of a man's lingam or a woman's yoni. Book a session today to experience the ultimate expression of personal body worship.

Yes, I thought. That's what I'm talking about: personal body worship. This is what I've been looking for. But who exactly are these goddesses, and what do they mean by a man's lingam and a woman's yoni?

I clicked on the button below marked *Lingam Massage*, and some black and white illustrations of a woman's hands massaging a man's erect penis appeared with a text box to the side.

The Sanskrit word for the male sex organ is Lingam, which is loosely translated as the 'Wand of Light'. In tantra, the Lingam is honored as the vessel that channels a man's creative energy and pleasure. The goal of the one-hour lingam massage is to caress the entire sensitive area including the testicles, perineum, and the Sacred Spot (prostate), allowing the man to surrender to a new, enlightened form of pleasure. Orgasm is not necessarily the goal, but it can be a welcome and pleasant side effect.

Orgasm isn't the goal? What the hell else do you expect the recipient to experience after one hour of massaging his dick, balls, and perineum?

But I liked the symbolism behind the words 'honoring' his sexual organ and enabling him to experience an 'enlightened form of pleasure'. Something told me that although orgasm wasn't the primary goal, most clients of this special form of massage therapy left with a very happy ending.

But it wasn't *male* pleasure and orgasm that I was interested in. I wanted these special massage goddesses to focus on administering a unique form of female-oriented pleasure. I clicked on the next button marked *Yoni Massage*, and some more erotic illustrations of a woman's hands massaging a woman's vulva appeared with another line of text below.

Yoni is the Sanskrit word for the vagina, which means the 'sacred temple' of a woman's body. During the yoni massage, the Goddess creates a unique space for the receiver to relax, from which she can enter a heightened state of arousal and ultimate pleasure. When orgasm does occur, it is often more expanded and more satisfying. While delivering a yoni massage, the giver should not expect anything in return, but simply allow the receiver to enjoy the experience and lose herself in the prolonged pleasure of being worshipped for the sexual person she is.

Fuck yes, I panted out loud. That's exactly what I wanted.

Someone to focus her attention entirely on my pleasure, who'd tease and torment me until I experienced the ultimate form of satisfaction. But even though I knew it would be an entirely one-way form of erotic stimulation, I still needed to be able to connect in some way with my partner. What did these so-called Goddesses look like? I wouldn't be able to truly immerse myself in the experience if I didn't find her attractive.

My gaze shifted to the menu on the sidebar, where a map displayed red pins showing the location of White Orchid goddesses in major cities throughout the United States. I clicked on the pin centered over Chicago and a photo of a pretty African-American girl named Violet appeared with a link for more details. The page opened with a picture of a dark, slender woman about my age wearing a skimpy leotard that hugged every inch of her lithe figure. It showed her leaning over a massage table while caressing the upper thighs of another woman lying face down with a small towel barely covering her upturned ass.

But it was *Violet's* ass that drew my immediate attention. Slender and curvy with separate volleyball-sized globes, the downward seam of her tights divided them into perfectly shaped spheres that made it look like her butt had been carved out of marble. I felt my panties begin to dampen as I imagined watching her sylphlike figure flexing and bending while she laid her hands on my body. I read the brief bio beside her picture, then my attention was drawn to the top of the page where a drop-down menu outlined her list of services.

I clicked on the Yoni Massage button, where some erotic pictures of Georgia O'Keefe floral artwork framed the detailed description of her ninety-minute intimate massage sessions. Although the verbiage referred to cryptic terms such as 'somatic pelvic floor exercises' and 'sexual energy cultivation techniques', I had little doubt, just as with the thinly-veiled symbolism of the Georgia O'Keefe paintings, where exactly she intended to focus her attention.

The massage sessions were provided at her personal studio and offered in blocks of four, each lasting roughly ninety minutes, with home assignments and email check-ins between sessions. There was no appointment form or payment link–only an email address where I was encouraged to leave a detailed message with my personal details and booking requests. I immediately clicked on the link and began composing a carefully worded message:

Violet,

I'm interested in booking a session for your one-on-one personal yoni massage. I work from home, so I'm available pretty much any time to meet at your studio, but weekends are my preferred time to concentrate on personal enrichment.

Please let me know the next available slot you have to fit me in. I look forward to learning more about your tantric exercises and experiencing your enlightened form of body worship.

Sincerely,

Jade

After I clicked send, I immediately winced at my not-so-subtle choice of words asking for a 'slot' to fit me in. But as I continued scanning her website page further describing the yoni massage procedure accompanied with more illustrations of the masseuse probing her client's orifices in various sexy positions, I pulled down my panties and thrust my fingers inside my hole, mimicking the Goddess's techniques.

You can press your fingers into my slot any way you like, I panted, running my eyes over her tight figure while I hunched over my keyboard feeling my pleasure beginning to rise...

2

———

By the time I finished coming down from my self-induced orgasm, I already had a new message notification in my inbox. I opened my mail and excitedly clicked on the message from GoddessViolet.

Jade,

Thank you for your inquiry regarding my services. I have an opening for yoni massage this Sunday at 2 p.m. if that works for you.

My fees are $600 for a four-massage package, with each massage offering a deeper and more intense stimulation of your sacred temple. I also offer a separate introductory massage for $200.

Please click on the PayPal link below to select and make advance payment for your preferred option. Once you complete the payment, I'll send another email with the address for my studio.

I look forward to our time together and feel blessed to share these transformative practices with you.

Love and blessings,

Violet

After reading her message, I sat back in my chair, contemplating my options. Six hundred bucks was a considerable sum, and although everything looked above-board on her website, I still couldn't be sure this wasn't some kind of scam. I clicked on the payment link and chose the two hundred dollar introductory option, then waited patiently for a reply with the additional details. It took a painfully long time for her to reply, but after she confirmed receipt of my payment and provided me with the location of her private studio, I breathed a sigh of relief.

For the next three days, I grew increasingly excited about my upcoming encounter, shaving my legs and armpits twice to make sure there'd be no unnecessary friction between any part of my skin and Violet's soft hands. Fortunately, my earlier laser hair treatment had already removed the last traces of any hairs from my mound and vulva. I must have come at least ten more times lying in front of my dressing room mirror imagining the sexy masseuse exploring every inch of my body.

By the time Sunday came around, my skin already felt like pins and needles in anticipation of Violet's tantric caresses. There was something about the idea of lying down and letting somebody bring me to the height of pleasure while she watched me writhe and moan in front of her that drove me crazy with desire. I'd always enjoyed having someone manually manipulate me to orgasm as much as oral or full-contact sex, knowing they could just sit back and savor my sexual response while concentrating all their energies on pleasing me.

When I drove to the address provided by Violet in her email, I was relieved to see it wasn't a cheap strip mall typical of those quick rub-and-tug operations. On the contrary, it was a beautiful luxury highrise with a commanding view of Lake Michigan only a few blocks away. If this was her primary source of income, I thought with a smile, she must run a pretty good book of business. I parked my car in the guest parking area then headed to the foyer where I buzzed the button for suite 2402.

"Hello?" a soft voice answered after a brief pause.

"It's Jade," I said. "I have a two p.m. appointment."

There was a loud buzz and I opened the unlocked entrance door then made my way to the elevator bank. I found it odd that she hadn't offered a more friendly greeting before buzzing me in, and during the long elevator ride to the twenty-fourth floor, I suddenly began to have second thoughts.

Just how safe is it to be walking into a stranger's highrise on the pretense of anonymous sex? I'd always wondered why most masseuses preferred to provide the service at their clients' homes rather than their own residence. Was this some kind of trap where someone just *pretending* to be Violet enticed me into his home only to hold me prisoner and have his way with me?

I was just about to tap out a warning message to my best friend Hannah on my phone when the elevator opened. The hallway was tastefully decorated with plush wool carpets, brightly illuminated wall sconces, and expensive brass door fixtures. I peered down the corridor in the direction of Violet's apartment near the end and put my phone back in my purse.

Fuck it, I said to myself, shaking the cobwebs out of my head. *If someone wanted to lure me into some kind of dangerous arrangement, they wouldn't do it in a place like this. Or give me their address, which I could easily share with my friends. She's probably doing this at her place as much to protect herself as me.*

When I reached her door, I paused to summon my courage, then tapped twice on the shiny lacquer surface.

Even the entrance to her 'studio' is upscale and enticing, I thought.

When the door swung open and I saw Violet peering out at me with a sweet smile, I breathed a sigh of relief. She was wearing a long silk kimono with a single white orchid nestled in the side of her upswept hair held back in a pretty bun. She was lighter-skinned than she appeared on the website, and with her smooth, caramel-colored complexion, large brown eyes and full sensuous lips, she reminded me of young Beyoncé.

"Good afternoon," she said standing to the side, motioning for me to enter her apartment.

When I walked through the door, she offered to take my coat then hung it in the adjacent closet. She led me to a large living room dominated by floor-to-ceiling windows displaying an unobstructed view of Lake Michigan, glistening like a sparkling jewel in the mid-afternoon sun. Her apartment was tastefully decorated in a minimal Japanese ethos, with a low-slung sectional sofa, large glass coffee table, and floral prints of George O'Keefe paintings on the wall. In the center of the room stood a long massage table covered in a white terrycloth towel.

My pussy fluttered at the sensual imagery of the setting and I peered at Violet with raised eyebrows.

"Wow," I said. "I've never had a massage in such a beautiful place. You have magnificent taste in your decor."

"Thank you," she said, motioning to a closed door a few feet behind her. "If you'd like to get changed, you can use my powder room. You'll find a cotton robe hanging on the back of the door."

"Thank you," I said, taking her cue to not waste any time and opening the door to the change room.

When I got inside, I closed it softly behind me, then leaned back against the partition while staring at myself in the oval mirror over the vanity.

Holy fuck! I mouthed the words silently, looking at myself in disbelief. Not only was Violet even more beautiful in person than she appeared on her website, her massage studio was something out of a fantasy dream. This wasn't some cheap massage parlor where you'd walk in for a quickie then hightail it out of there so as not to be seen. This was more like the luxury upscale spa Hannah and I'd gone to a few months earlier where we were feted and spoiled for much of the day. The difference was that in *this* place, I had both the masseuse *and* the exquisite surroundings all to myself for the next ninety minutes.

As I began disrobing and neatly folding my clothes on the tasteful sidestand to the left side of the sink, I began singing the melody to the Beyoncé song Irreplaceable.

To the left, to the left
To the left, to the left
Everything you own in the box to the left

In the closet that's my stuff, yes
If I bought it please don't touch...

I'd always thought the singer was one of the most beautiful women I'd ever seen. I must have watched the sexy video of that song a hundred times, fantasizing that it was me squatting over her sexy legs while she sat in front of her makeup mirror in a slinky negligee. And now I had the chance to relive my fantasy with a dead ringer who was about to touch me in the most intimate way.

After I removed all my clothes, I looked at myself in the mirror appraising my naked, freshly primped body. I still had a pretty sexy figure for a woman in her mid-thirties, with firm plump breasts sitting high on my chest, a narrow, toned waist, and long slender legs. I wondered how much attention the *front* of my body would get from Violet during this first encounter. I knew most masseuses only attended to the back of their clients' bodies while focusing on relaxing and removing the knots from their muscles, rather than stimulating the more erogenous areas of their figures.

No matter, I said to myself, slipping my arms through the sleeves of the waffle-patterned robe hanging on the back of the door and tying the belt loosely around my waist before swinging the door open.

Either way, I planned to give my sexy masseuse ample access to my 'sacred places', whether I was lying face down or face up.

3

———

When I emerged from the powder room, I was surprised to see that Violet had removed her robe and was preparing her tools on a side table next to the massage table. Instead of the long silk robe, she was now wearing a thin cotton tank top with matching white cotton tights. The tight fabric clung to every curvature of her body and when she swung around to greet me, I gasped audibly when I saw her full figure for the first time.

Her breasts were petite, but they had an exquisite elongated, scooped shape that made the front of her skimpy t-shirt tent and bulge with prominent sensuous darts poking out from her hardened nipples. Her thin cotton tights also left a minimal amount to the imagination, with the soft fabric flowing over her flat pelvis and sensuously curved hips to her shapely, well-toned legs. I could see the cleft from the slit of her pussy as the fabric clung to her like a second skin, daring me to soak up her body with my wide eyes. In a way, it was even *more* erotic to see her cloaked in the soft white covering barely concealing her dark areolas and sexy camel toe, beckoning for me to approach her closer.

"May I take your robe?" she said, holding out her Madonna-toned arms in front of her.

"Um–yes," I stammered, momentarily pulled out of my trance.

I turned around and she softly pulled the robe off my shoulders then placed it on a side table beside the sofa. I peered at the massage table inquisitively, then turned back around to face Violet.

"Do you want me to lie face up or down?" I said, unsure of the protocol with this new procedure.

"Let's go face down to start," she smiled, extending her arm toward the table.

I lifted my right knee and climbed onto the bench, extending my legs straight down behind me. There was no customary hole at the head of the table where I'd normally place my face to relax my neck muscles, so I turned my head to peer out over the wide expanse of sparkling blue water. As soon as I saw the soothing picture of the gently lapping waves and reflected sunshine, I immediately began to feel the sexual tension ebb away. Whether this was by design or incidental, I wasn't sure. But for a few brief moments, I forgot about the primary purpose for my visit and flitted my eyelids in sublime bliss. Even if I just had to lie here watching this spectacular scenery for an hour and a half, it would almost be worth the two hundred dollar price of admission.

But it didn't take long for my *other* senses to be awakened as Violet opened her scented bottles of massage oil and the smell of jasmine and chamomile filled my nostrils. I breathed the heavenly scent in as I expanded my lungs and my chest rose and fell gently on the padded table. I could hear the sound of oil dribbling into her hands as she turned one of the bottles upside-down, then rubbed them together slowly. My pussy quivered knowing that she would soon lay her moistened hands on my skin, and I extended my arms to my side, inviting her to begin touching me.

I was a little disappointed when she started at the foot of the table with my feet, but I smiled peering up at the large analog clock hanging on the near wall, knowing she had a full ninety minutes to explore the rest of my body. I relaxed the muscles tensing in my shoulders and buttocks, happy to bide my time while she worked her way up toward my waiting temple.

As she separated each of my toes between her slippery fingers and kneaded them softly and sensuously, I was tempted to talk to her to break the awkward silence. But I knew from previous massages that masseuses preferred to work in silence, encouraging their clients to relax and let all the external distractions melt away. The whole point of a massage was to concentrate on the soothing feeling of being caressed, and I had no intention of disrupting Violet's mojo at the outset of our erotic encounter.

But that didn't stop me from letting my mind wander to all manner of sexual imagery while she squeezed and kneaded my extremities. As she pulled her fingers slowly down each of my toes from the ball of my foot to the toenails, I imagined it was my *clit* she was pinching between her fingers while she stroked my hard shaft and teased the tip of my nub. Whenever she slipped her fingers between my toes, I channeled her inserting her slender digits between my dripping *labia*, feeling my wet tunnel gripping her tightly. And when she grabbed my feet and pressed her thumbs against my soles while she pulled my toes against her washboard-hard tummy, I imagined toe-fucking her pussy while she gripped me in the throes of passion.

By the time her fingers moved to my ankles and began working their way up the inside of my calves, I was already soaking wet while I unconsciously ground my mound into the moistening towel beneath me. I spread my legs apart, inviting Violet to move closer to my apex, but she seemed in no hurry to attend to my quivering pussy. Instead, she wrapped her fingers around the curvature of my calves, rubbing them softly and slowly with her warm, slippery hands. Unlike the firm and sometimes painful kneading of my muscles that most masseurs were accustomed to administering, her touch was always light and sensuous, focused instead on titillating and stimulating every square inch of my skin. Reflecting back on what I'd read on the White Orchid website, I knew that she had a plan for eventually reaching my 'sacred temple', with the goal of heightening my arousal to achieve the 'ultimate pleasure'.

I tried to relax my arms and the rest of my body while she worked her way further up the inside of my thighs, but I couldn't help curling my upturned fingers in a come-hither motion in the direction of my aching sex. But just as her thumbs began probing the edges of my tumescent lips, she suddenly shifted position and moved up to the *head* of the table, placing her moist hands on my shoulders and upper back. This time I could detect the scent of my own juices intermingled with the aromatic massage oil as her hands slid over my pliant skin, and I turned my head away from the direction of the lake to watch Violet more closely.

As she stood to the side of the long table to gain better access to my upper back, I stared at her crotch while she leaned and stroked my shoulders and neck softly. The fabric of the white cotton tights pulled and stretched as she swayed her body overtop of me, and I could feel my mouth beginning to water while I imagined sucking her sweet pussy into my mouth. She must have known what was on my mind while she did this, because she hesitated for the longest time pressing the bottom of her undergarments sensuously against the padded corner of the table while she moved her hands progressively further down my back.

I was disappointed when she shifted position once again, denying me ready viewing access to her lower body, but I smiled when I noticed a small wet spot forming in the seam of her pants below her vulva. This time, she moved her hips directly over the top of my head while she extended her arms further down the center of my back toward my flexing buttocks. She placed her thumbs together, sliding them sensuously down the valley in the center of my back, and I lifted my ass, trying to narrow the distance between her probing fingers and my puckering lips. Making my torment all the more intense, while she pressed her palms further down my back in a series of forward-and-back movements, she gently pushed her pubis against the back of my head.

Whether she was doing this for her own amusement or mine, I couldn't be sure. But it took every ounce of my willpower not to lift my head and clamp onto her pussy like a wild boar catching its prey after a long chase through the underbrush. By now I was panting heavily, and she must have felt my breath on her upper thighs straddling either side of my head. As she neared the small of my back with her probing thumbs, I tilted my hips as far as I could in her direction, pointing the cleft of my ass directly up toward her face. The further she probed down my body, the closer her torso leaned over the surface of my back, until I could feel her pointy breasts and hard nipples touching my skin.

I groaned quietly, begging her to press her fingers into my crack. When she finally did, my cheeks quivered, anticipating her reaching my aching sex. Instead, she wrapped her hands around the globes of my ass and squeezed them firmly, tantalizing me with the tips of her fingers as they touched the outside edges of my external labia. I grunted more loudly and swiveled my butt in circles, signaling to her that I was desperate for her to administer to my yoni as her website had promised.

Recognizing my impatience, Violet released the pressure on my buttocks and threaded her thumbs into my crevasse, rolling them softly over my puckering rosebud. I groaned like a cat in heat when I felt her touch my sensitive tissue, and I spread my legs further apart to make it easier for her to slide her fingers over my crescent toward my swollen lips and buzzing clit. As she leaned her torso more firmly atop my back and pressed her mound harder against my moistening head, she began angling her palms inward, caressing the outside of my dripping labia with the tips of her fingers while she continued stimulating my sphincter with her thumbs. The combined sensation of her fingers probing my anus and the edges of my widening gash simultaneously was driving me crazy with passion, but she still hadn't touched me in the most sensitive area that would lead me toward a much-needed orgasm.

When she finally began pressing her fingers further down my crease toward my flaring slit and pinching my folds between her index and middle finger, sliding them sensuously along the length of my engorged labia, I hummed a sigh of pleasure knowing it wouldn't be long before Violet finally brought me to sexual nirvana. But just as she began pressing her digits into my pulsing hole, I heard a soft chime and she withdrew her hands from my private areas as quickly as she had entered.

I twisted my head to peer up at her inquisitively, and she turned around to face the large clock on the wall while reaching over to the side table to dry off her dripping hands with a small towel. I looked up at the clock and was horrified to see the large hand pointing straight down, marking the completion of our session at three-thirty. Somehow, in all the heat of the slow buildup, I'd completely lost track of time.

"It appears that our time's up for today," Violet said nonchalantly. "I hope you enjoyed your introduction to tantric massage."

So that's her game, I thought, shaking my head in dismay. *She suckers me in with this so-called introductory session, driving me to the point of near-delirium then sends me packing just as I'm about to get off. Talk about a honey trap.*

I was pissed beyond belief, but the sight of Violet standing before me with the front of her cotton ensemble drenched in a combination of massage oil and my own sensual juices soon made me forget about her questionable business practice. The wetness had made her t-shirt nearly transparent, and I gawked like a newborn baby at her large brown medallions and pointed nipples pressing against the thin fabric. Even the front of her *tights* was soaking wet, pulled up between her flaring labia at the base of her mound. I wasn't sure if it was from her own juices released while she was grinding against my head or from the sweat pouring out of my hair as I got increasingly turned on, but it didn't matter. All I could think about was continuing her program of tantric massage and getting as close as I could to this beautiful goddess again as soon as possible. She had me hooked like a fish, and she knew it.

"How soon are you available for another session?" I asked meekly, sitting up on top of the giant wet spot I'd created in the middle of the massage table.

4

After my equally titillating and frustrating initial massage session with Violet, I had to wait a whole week to see her again. In the intervening time, I vacillated between fuming over the disappointing ending she'd delivered and reliving her slow but intense buildup. Even though I didn't experience my usual climactic finish, I hadn't felt so turned on for so long in a very long time.

During my subsequent masturbation sessions, instead of rushing toward orgasm in the usual manner, I brought myself close to the edge repeatedly, resisting the temptation to fall over the precipice and quickly come down from my highs. There was something strangely liberating about being able to sustain such intense pleasure for as long as I wanted without always feeling the need for the final payoff. If this was what tantric sex was all about, I was rapidly becoming a passionate proponent of the mysterious practice.

By the time the following Sunday rolled around, my entire body was buzzing from my extended edging sessions, and I was eager to feel Violet's magic hands upon me once again. When I arrived at her studio and she opened the door, she was already wearing her sensuous white cotton undergarments, and we wasted no time getting started.

"Face up or face down?" I asked succinctly after shedding my street clothes in her powder room.

"Down," she said, equally matter-of-factly.

I climbed up on the padded massage table and extended my arms behind me, turning my head to peer out at the calming expanse of blue water extending out to the horizon. This time I was determined to relax and simply enjoy the voyage Violet took me on, realizing this process was far more about the journey than the destination.

She began once again at the foot of my body, but this time, instead of clasping both of my feet at the same time, she focused her attention only on my left foot, caressing the hard instep and my soft sole with gentle circular motions of her moistened hands. I could smell the gentle aroma of apple intermingled with the other scented oils, and my mouth began to water once again imagining myself lapping up her juices as she approached my erogenous zones. The combination of her firm kneading of my dorsal bone and the soft pressing of her digits into the pliant flesh of my sole reminded me of the sensation of a lover running her hands down over my pubis into the loose folds of my vulva. I purred like a kitten soaking up the exquisite slowness and eroticism of her touch.

As she shifted toward the top of my foot, instead of moving up the insides of my lower legs, this time she rolled her hands over the bump on the outside of my ankle like a pitcher softening up a base-ball before delivering it to the opposing batter. Except in this case, I was transfixed by her pre-delivery ritual, already losing focus on why I was hunched over the plate, watching her graceful movement in the reflection of the big picture window.

When she began running her hands up along the outside edge of my leg, I couldn't help flexing my calves and thighs in autonomic response to her sensuous touch. As she approached my downturned pelvis, she slipped her fingers under my hips, tracing the curved ridge along the top of my crest. Although her fingers never got closer than a few inches from my tingling mound and pussy, the feeling of her sliding her fingers over my hard bone was one of the most erotic sensations I'd ever experienced.

I tilted my body a few inches away from her to give her some more space, and she pushed me further onto my side, with the front of my body now facing her. I turned my face to peer in her direction and was happy to see her newly oil-stained bodysuit displaying her beautiful brown skin underneath.

As she began running her palms over the side indentation of my waist, I could feel the goose bumps on my skin beginning to rise while I watched her tits jiggling in her tight tank-top. Although the upper part of her ensemble wasn't as wet as the lower portion, I could see her large brown areolas and protruding peaks through the light-colored fabric, daring me not to ogle them like a star-struck fangirl.

When she placed her palms on my quivering tummy and began moving her hands toward my mashed-together breasts, my mouth opened unconsciously, desperately wanting to suck on her succulent teats. I could feel my own tips hardening the closer she got to my mounds, and when she encircled them with her palms, rolling the tips between her thumbs and forefingers, I gasped at how delicious it felt. I'd heard rumors how some women unconsciously reached orgasm from breast-feeding their babies, and now I understood how sensitive this part of the body could get when properly stimulated and caressed.

I groaned as Violet cupped my breasts, teasing me ever-so-gently with her warm, oily hands and soft fingertips. I probably could have come if she'd continued twisting and rolling my nubs for much longer, but just as before, she moved on just as I was nearing the turning point. I was sad to see her take her attention away from my engorged tits, but what she did next soon had me wishing she'd climb on top of me and have done with me.

Tilting my upper body further back, she pressed her palms firmly against my upper chest while she spread her fingers apart approaching my neck. As she encircled my narrow isthmus, I tilted my head up, and she squeezed my throat gently with the open palms of her hands. I'd never felt so vulnerable and sexually charged having someone else's hands on me, and I grunted like a wild animal lost in the clutches of a predator. While she was doing this, I could have sworn that her nipples pressed even further out against the flimsy fabric of her cotton t-shirt, and I detected a slight upward curl of her lips as she grasped me in the delicate embrace.

Was she getting just as turned on as I was from all this sexy imagery?

If so, I was more than happy for her to take whatever further advantage she desired of me, feeling my body's sexual energy rapidly rounding second base. But she obviously had no intention of suffocating me, and her hands continued their upward momentum as they rolled over my chin and jawline. When her apple-scented fingers moved next to my lips, I opened my mouth and she curled them into my cavity while I sucked on the tasty juices and kneaded her phalanges playfully with the tips of my teeth.

Two can play this game, I smiled, preventing her fingers from pulling out of me while I glared up at her with piercing eyes.

Instead of trying to remove her trapped fingers from my mouth, she curled her thumbs around the dripping edges of my lips, tracing a line around the raised edges, mimicking the caress of my outer labia. When I unconsciously groaned from the symbolism of her erotic touch, she pulled her fingers out from my loosened grip, then glided them up the side of my cheeks toward the bottom of my ears, curling them around their perimeter and pinching her fingers around the outside edges.

By now, I was moaning like a cat in heat and twisting my body in sexual abandon, eager for her to take me anyway she could. Her slow, teasing buildup was driving me crazy with desire, and I clasped the sides of her forearms, trying to pull her toward me. But she tensed the muscles in her strong arms as she resisted my attempt, running her oily fingers through my hair and over the back of my scalp. I didn't care for a millisecond that she was making a mess of my carefully coiffed hair while I looked up at her, begging her to fuck me.

Seeming to acknowledge my torment, she pulled her hands away from my face and moved them slowly across the side of my shoulder, tracing a line down the side of my arm with the lightest of touches, making my hairs stand up on end. When she reached my hand, she interlaced her fingers with mine, then lifted my arm, pressing it over my head. Then she clasped the underside of my upturned limb, threading her other hand with equal tenderness up the soft skin on the other side. When she reached my armpit, she paused for a moment, massaging the indented space firmly with her oily thumbs, now even further moistened from the saliva of my mouth.

"Oh God," I moaned, amazed at how her touching me in every place other than the most sensitive areas of my body could make me feel this electrified.

With my arm still held gently over the top of my head and lying pinned on my side, my breasts were pulled off-center and rolling atop one another, creating a new kind of sensation I hadn't felt before as my oiled flesh rubbed sensuously together. All the time I was moaning with every hair on my body standing on end, Violet watched me with her big doe eyes and glistening lips. I wanted desperately for her to lean over and suck my bullets into her mouth, bringing me to orgasm just like the breastfeeding mothers I'd heard about, but I knew that was too much to hope for at this still-early juncture.

She angled my arm gently back down onto my side, placing it softly on the table in front of me, then traced a line all the way down the hourglass-shaped side of my back, up and over the curvature of my ass and down the back of my upper thigh, pausing to caress the tender space behind the back of my knee. Then she pronated her hand and pulled my knee slowly up toward my hips, forcing my legs into a bent-knee scissor position.

I was now lying on my side on the massage table, drenched in massage oil, with my legs splayed into a side-split position, with the glistening gash of my billowy cunt freely displayed for her viewing pleasure. I could feel my juices pouring out of me while her gaze turned toward my slit, dripping over my engorged lips and down the front of my lower thigh. I felt incredibly sexy and exposed in this compromising position, and if she'd so much as *blown* anywhere in the direction of my flaring snatch, I'm sure I would have come in a nanosecond.

Realizing I was now about as aroused as I was ever going to be, Violet slowly rolled her palm over the arc of my upturned hip and turned her hand sideways, curving the side of it softly between the crack of my ass. The feeling of her oily hand slicing my cleft like a soft bread knife was another sensation I'd never felt before, and I tilted my pelvis toward her, desperately trying to bring her hand closer to my aching clit.

Clearly trying to extend my agony as long as possible, she waved the side of her hand gently up and down the length of my crease, stimulating my anus and the lower reaches of my opening with a slow, measured touch. Growing increasingly impatient, I glanced up at the wall and noticed that it was three-fifteen. There was only fifteen minutes left for Violet to bring me to the peak of pleasure. I was all for the idea of extending this intense feeling as long as possible, but sometimes a girl just needed to get off.

Noticing me peering up at the clock, Violet opened her hand and pressed her fingers further down toward my slit. When she reached my opening, I was elated when she curled them inside me, pressing her three middle fingers deep inside my tunnel. I groaned in excitement, angling my hips to extend them as far inside me as possible. For a few brief moments, I was content to simply hump her fingers embedded inside me, but the angle of her hand reaching over from the side made it difficult for her to stimulate my G-spot in the usual manner.

I twisted my hips in a circular motion trying to angle her hand in the direction of my most sensitive part and we she realized what I was attempting to do, she began flexing her index finger forward and back, finally caressing the magic spot on the inside of my pussy. I groaned in delight at the pleasant sensation, but something was still missing. As much as I was enjoying the feeling of her fingering my hole and teasing my G-spot, I still needed some direct contact with my clit.

I tilted my hips further upward, sliding her pinky up the outside edge of my labia and when I felt it make contact with my tingling gland, I groaned deeply, finally beginning to feel the familiar pangs of my orgasm approaching. Seeking to add more pleasure to my rapidly building excitement, Violet simultaneously extended her thumb toward my tight pucker as she circled her pinky over my swollen bulb.

Fuck yes, I thought, growling like a wildcat. Finally, she's hitting all the right buttons. I could feel my orgasm rapidly approaching, and I gripped the sides of the massage table while I stared at Violet's sexy tits pressing against the soft fabric of her t-shirt, preparing for the inevitable release. But just before I passed the moment of no return, the dreaded chime sounded again, and Violet paused with her hand deeply embedded in my tunnel. For a brief moment, I thought she was going to continue to finish me off, and I groaned when she began to pull her hand out of me.

What the fuck? I thought, panting wildly. *This isn't tantric massage—it's tantric torture! How can she do this to me, knowing how much I needed the ultimate release her website had clearly alluded to?* As she slowly began to clean up, I couldn't help asking the obvious question.

"That was wonderful," I said, sitting up reluctantly. "But when are you going to take me to that magical place of enlightenment your website promised?"

"Remember, the purpose of tantric massage isn't just about reaching sexual climax," she said, wiping the oil nonchalantly from her hands. "It's an opportunity for you to connect with your inner feelings and extend the pleasurable sensations to their maximum degree."

"But your website suggested that when orgasm is achieved this way, it is often more expanded and intense than usual. Isn't that one of the sensations you help your clients achieve at some point in this process?"

"Yes," she said. "But remember, you still have two more sessions in your scheduled package. Most of the pleasure is experienced during the slow and extended build-up."

"Okay," I said. "But I don't know if I'm going to be able to hold out much longer. What can I look forward to during my next session?"

"At stage three, the process will become more interactive, with closer contact between the two of us, adding an extra level of stimulation and excitement. I think you'll find the next stage in your journey takes you to an entirely new level of fulfilment."

I wasn't entirely sure what she meant by more *interactive*, but if it involved more body contact with her magnificent figure, I knew that would be more than enough to allow me to achieve my ultimate goal.

"You're a very demanding coach," I smiled. "I'm looking forward to improving my batting average the next time around."

"Next time we'll see if we can deliver some *home runs*," she nodded, adding to my athletic analogy.

5

I had to wait another week to see Violet again, and in the intervening time I came many times reliving the exhilarating experience of her caressing my most sensitive regions. At the last session she'd finally gotten around to touching my clit, but she'd left me hanging at the edge of another powerful orgasm. I was beginning to grow tired of this tantric 'edging' technique. After all the teasing and intense build-up, I was shaking so much by the time she finished that I could barely walk out of her apartment and back to my car.

At my next session I was determined to get off even if I had to grab hold of her and mash my pussy into her face until I climaxed. She'd promised that this massage would be more interactive, and as I drove to her apartment, my mind raced with all manner of exciting visions. Would she finally suck my throbbing pearl into her pretty mouth? Was she going to mount me and grind her sexy body against mine? Was it too much to hope for her to take off her skimpy leotard and let me see her glorious naked figure unencumbered for the first time?

By the time I got to her building, my panties were already soaked through imagining all the different ways we could interact in the ninety minutes we had together. But when she opened the door to her apartment, I was disappointed to see her clad once again in her cotton tights. I'd hoped we could jump-start this process of interactive discovery by being able to touch her in the way she'd been touching me. I'd spent long hours dreaming about how I could tease and drive her crazy with desire before finishing the two of us off in a climactic crescendo.

This time, I didn't even bother putting on the robe on the back of the change room door. Instead, I pranced out into the middle of her living room stark naked, not wanting to waste a precious second getting started.

"Face up?" I said, glancing at the massage table standing in the middle of her room framed by her floor-to-ceiling windows and the beautiful expanse of Lake Michigan extending for miles into the horizon.

"Down," she said matter-of-factly.

No worries, I thought, taking my time to give her an unobstructed view of my glistening snatch as I lifted my knee to climb up onto the table. *If this massage is anything like the last one, there'll still be plenty of chances for her to access my private parts.*

As I lay down on the padded table, I turned my head in the direction of the lake and closed my eyes with a contented smile. There was something incredibly exciting about the idea of lying naked on a platform designed for no other purpose than caressing another person's body and waiting to see exactly where and how my paramour intended to arouse me. As I listened to Violet preparing her materials on the side table next to my stand, my entire body tingled in preparation for her erotic touch.

But this time, the first thing I felt touch my body wasn't her fingers. It was a warm flat stone, placed between my shoulder blades, just below the nape of my neck. While it was a pleasant sensation, I was disappointed to find her resorting to traditional massage techniques. I was eager for her to get on with the erotic aspect of the massage, mindful of how quickly our previously scheduled time had slipped away from us.

But as she began to place successive hot stones down the ridge of my spine in the direction of my butt, I could feel my pulse quickening. Each stone seemed warmer than the one before, and by the time she reached the small of my back, my buttocks were quivering imagining what she planned to do next. The stones were hot enough to make my skin burn momentarily, but soft and gentle enough to send a shiver down my spine.

Violet paused for a moment, knowing my mind was racing with what she intended to do with the stones. When I felt her place the next one on its side and begin sliding it toward the crack of my ass, I tilted my pelvis toward her. She drew the edge of the rock into the top of my slit, then pulled it back toward the base of my spine, making me squirm in anticipation.

The idea of her caressing my underside with these exotic stones was something I'd never even considered. Unlike my cold, plastic- or silicone-covered sex toys, this massage aid was definitely new and unique. Of course, the fact that there was an incredibly sexy person on the other end of them teasing and caressing me *also* elevated the experience beyond my usual self-administered masturbatory sessions.

As Violet continued to tease me by sliding the edge of the oiled stone in and out of the top of my crease, I moaned and flexed my buttocks in a vain attempt to clamp the object and encourage her to move it further down in the direction of my pussy. When she finally slid it over my quivering rosebud, I squealed at the sublime sensation of the warm, slippery rock against my sensitive skin.

I'd never been particularly excited about anal sex, but the feeling of this sexy goddess probing my most private area with this smooth oblong object was something new altogether. The shape of oil-covered stone seemed perfectly designed to slide through my fissure, now thoroughly greased and ready for whatever she had in mind. I resolved there and then to add these erotic rocks to my repertoire of sex toys and experiment with them at home as often as I could.

When Violet began sliding the stone lower toward the base of my slit, I could feel the oil dripping down and over my folds, causing me to groan more loudly. I spread my legs apart, encouraging her to go lower, and when she dipped the smooth edge of the stone into my slit, I grunted, pressing my mound hard against the table. As she began to sensuously probe the outer edge of my pussy with the object, I rocked my hips in tandem with her movement, feeling the pleasure beginning to rise within my body.

She pressed the stone further into my gap, and for a moment I thought she was going to release it and let it float inside me like some kind of oversize, heated Ben-Wa ball. As much as that might have increased my pleasure by placing it closer to my G-spot, she seemed determined to maintain control and continue torturing me while I humped the massage table ever more frantically.

But once again, just as I was approaching the peak of my pleasure, she withdrew the stone from my hole and placed it flat against my opening. I glanced in the reflection of her living room window and saw her peering at my dripping pussy and quivering ass, then she looked up, smiling back at my reflection.

"Time to turn over," she said softly.

In the three sessions we'd spent together so far, we'd barely strung three or four complete sentences together. But somehow, this strong, silent treatment only added to the excitement of lying helplessly in her hands.

"My pleasure," I said, flipping over like a fish out of water at the knowledge that she'd finally have direct, unfettered access to my aching clit.

But instead of moving the stone further up my channel toward my buzzing gland, she reached over to her side table for a new stone, dipping it in a bowl of hot oil. When I felt it dripping on my bare mound and stomach as she lifted it over the surface of my body, I gasped at how delicious it felt. While I stared up at her with pleading eyes, she took the edge of the searing stone and began tracing it softly around the edges of my areolas.

I peered down the front of my body and saw my nipples standing firmer than I'd ever seen them before. Whether this was from my skin recoiling at the sensation of the hot stone touching it or from the heightened sense of arousal I was feeling seeing Violet watching me as my body responded to her touch, I wasn't sure. But either way, I was in heaven as I tilted my head back and raised my chest up toward her angelic face. I closed my eyes, hoping this was just a prelude to her finally climbing up on the massage table with me, as she'd alluded to her final comments at our last session.

But for now at least, she seemed content on teasing me by sliding the side of the stone around the perimeter of my areolas, then softly over the tips of my tingling teats until I was writhing uncontrollably on the massage table. Recognizing how turned on this was making me, she alternated between teasing my nipples with the edge of the stone and laying it flat against the surface of my breasts while rolling it softly over my soft and pliant flesh.

While she was tormenting me with this erotic dance of warm stone caresses between my breasts, I noticed Violet grinding the base of her mound against the side of the massage table next to me. It took every ounce of my willpower not to reach up and pull her down on top of me where I could properly fuck her. But I was prepared to give her a little longer, knowing that she'd promised to deliver a 'home run' after our last session together. I still wanted to feel her build me up to the height of pleasure, then allow me to release my pent-up excitement in one final, gigantic orgasm while she watching me writhing and moaning inches before her eyes.

After stimulating my nipples and breasts for a few minutes, she finally began rolling the stone down the front of my quivering stomach toward my aching pussy. I smiled at the inventive ways she used the device to tease me, with the rolling wheel adding to the imagery of her steering toward my final destination. But when she got to my bare mound, instead of rolling the stone further down toward my tingling clit, she paused over my hard pubis, flattening it so I could feel its full radiant heat on my trembling pelvis.

As she swiped the warm pebble closer and closer to the base of my mound and my buzzing clit, I lifted my hips higher and higher off the surface of the massage table. Desperately wanting her to place the rock over my tingling gland, I glanced up at the clock, wondering if she was going to leave me hanging once again on the edge of release.

When she noticed me looking up at the clock and seeing we only had ten minutes remaining in our session, she suddenly grasped my ankles, pulling my body down the massage table toward her as she spread my legs apart. I looked up at her in surprise, and she smiled back at me while she calmly replaced the lukewarm stone with two hotter black stones. Then she placed each one on the inside of my ankles, slowly sliding them up the inside of my calves and thighs.

While she did this, I spread my legs even further apart, giving her an eagle-eye view of my gaping vulva. It must have been a tantalizing sight with her face only inches away from my splayed pussy, dripping down the sides of my thighs and ass cheeks in a virtual cascade. As I twisted and turned my hips, begging her to touch my cunny directly with the rocks to put me out of my misery, she turned them once again onto their sides and pressed them hard against the outside edges of my labia while she slid them forward and back along my opening.

With each rhythmic movement, she pressed the stones closer and closer together, until they were sandwiched between the palms of her hands. As I lay before her in my prostrated position with my legs splayed and my knees bent, she began rolling and pressing the stones deeper into my slit. When I felt them approach the top of my folds and touch my clit, I gasped, lifting my hips even higher above the table.

As the joined tablets rolled over my nub and along the sides of my erect shaft, Violet eased up on the pressure. The hollow created between the two rounded stones acted as a perfect conduit for my engorged gland, and she smiled while she teased my clit with gentle forward and back rocking motions. With my hips now pitching and rolling in escalating need, she finally separated the stones and placed one of them flat atop my burning jewel. At first, she just held it there for a moment while I reveled in the exquisite feeling of the smooth, hot rock radiating its energy into my core.

But when she began to turn the rock in a slow twisting motion against my glans, I whinnied in pleasure at the unique feeling of the warm object pressing against my aperture. As I began to feel my pleasure beginning to rise like an oncoming tidal wave, Violet slid the other rock vertically into my tunnel, rolling the edge of it against the inside front surface of my pussy on my G-spot. The combination of the sustained brushing of the warm stone on my burning bean and the gentle rolling of the stone over the underside of my clit soon brought me once again to the brink of pleasure.

As I peered down toward Violet, I noticed the front of her tights were now soaked with a large wet spot while she ground the base of her pussy against the corner of the massage table. Seeing her enjoying herself almost as much as me while she watched me grunting and groaning under her ministrations soon took me over the edge. As I felt my orgasm begin to consume my body in one cataclysmic earthquake, I gripped the side of the massage table with both hands, and jetted my pent-up juices all over Violet's pretty tank-top while I stared at her pointy tits as she slumped over the base of the table in a simultaneous climax with me.

I must have remained in this epileptic state for a minute or longer, because by the time I finally came down from my intense climax, my entire body was quivering in exhaustion. When I peered back up at Violet, she was still hunched over the end of the massage table, breathing heavily in her own post-orgasmic bliss. This wasn't exactly what I envisioned by her cryptic comment at the end of our last massage session when she suggested the next two sessions would be more 'interactive', but I smiled knowing I still had one more appointment remaining in my scheduled package.

As I peered back up at the clock realizing our time had finally run out, my mind was already racing ahead to my next chance to touch this gorgeous African-American goddess flesh-to-flesh.

6

Thankfully, I only had to wait three more days for my next appointment with Violet. Whether this was because she was just as excited as me to explore the next step in our rapidly escalating engagement, I wasn't sure. But one thing was certain. This last session was going to be 'interactive' in the fullest sense of the word, whether she intended it or not. After we'd shared a brief moment of mutual intimacy, there was no way I was going to let her off the hook with another one-way massage encounter. I'd fulfilled my goal of lying passive while she brought me to the height of passion manually. Now it was time for us to merge our bodies together and experience a whole *new* kind of tantric pleasure.

I could barely sleep during the intervening nights as I lay awake planning all the different ways we could stimulate each other and achieve the penultimate pleasure her website had alluded to. Although the first three sessions had been exciting with each one increasing my degree of arousal, there were still plenty of ways I could think of to ramp up the action and give both of us an opportunity to reach our maximum potential. I'd read somewhere that most people took less than eight minutes to complete the act of sexual congress. An hour and a half of dedicated erotic touching was more than enough time for each of us to enjoy an incredible build-up and an earth-shaking climax. And I had every intention of giving Violet just as good as I got.

When I arrived at her apartment at the scheduled time, we went through the usual preliminaries, with me lying dutifully facedown on her terrycloth-covered massage table. But this time, instead of pouring the massage oil into her hands and proceeding to rub me down like the previous times, she tipped the bottle of warm liquid over my ankles and drizzled it in two long, sensuous streams up the back of my legs, curving over the arch of my buttocks and leaving a small puddle in the small of my back.

This was new, I thought, feeling the liquid slowly spreading over my ass cheeks as it flowed into my crack and dribbled down my cleft onto my puckering lips and tingling clit. *But why so much–and why only on my legs?*

When she placed the palms of her hands on my ankles and began to slide them up the back of my legs, spreading the oil evenly over my calves and thighs, I wasn't sure what she was up to. But when I heard the table suddenly creak and the bottom of the cushion indenting from a heavy weight, I squirmed my hips in delight. She was finally getting up on the massage table where we could press our bodies together and experience a different kind of body contact!

As she spread my feet apart, I felt her kneel between my ankles, then she placed her palms on my skin, pressing them firmly into my flesh while her thumbs teased and tickled the inside of my legs. When she reached the top of my thighs, her oily fingers circled tantalizingly at the edge of my opening, then she spread my cheeks wide apart while she squeezed my globes. I could feel my pucker being stretched and twisted while she did this, and I wondered just how much she was enjoying seeing me spread apart for her viewing pleasure.

I shimmied my ass, encouraging her to touch me more closely, then she slid her thumbs over my rosebud, rubbing it sensuously in little concentric circles. When I squeezed my buttocks, grinding my mound into the padded table, she pressed my legs together and straddled the back of my thighs with her knees. I could feel her mound pressing against the back of my ass, and I tilted it up, encouraging her to hump me while she stimulated herself.

She raised her hands off my butt, and I heard the sound of clothing rustling behind me. When I peered in the reflection of the glass and saw her pulling off her tank-top, I tilted my head, struggling to peer at naked torso. I'd waited almost three weeks to see her undressed, and I didn't want to miss one precious second of soaking up her gorgeous body. But she leaned forward, pressing my shoulder blades back down onto the cushion, then she dipped her tits into the warm puddle of oil still resting in the small of my back. When I felt her hard nipples on my skin, I groaned, trying vainly to reach around my sides to caress her beautiful ass. But she seemed to have other plans, sweeping my hands to the side and forcing my arms back to the side of my body. Then she arched her spine, pressing her mounds into my flesh as she slowly crawled over my ass.

Feeling her whole body touching mine for the first time was sublime, and I squirmed and mewed while she body-fucked me with her writhing figure. When her head reached my shoulders, I could feel her cool breath on the back of my neck, and I turned my face in the other direction, hoping to meet her lips. But she continued sliding up my body as her tits separated over my nape, where I saw her dark areolas and long nipples tantalizing me beside my cheek. I flapped my mouth open like a fish lunging for a lure, but she kept her berries just out of my reach.

I could feel the heat of her body against mine and the aroma of her exotic scent commingled with the massage oils, and when she moved slightly higher pinning my waist to the table under her hips, she rubbed her oily breasts over the back of my head. I thrashed my head wildly from side to side, not minding for a second that she was making another mess of my freshly washed hair. When she leaned over and rested her elbows on the pad beside my ears, I could feel her wet crotch humping the small of my back, soaking up the rest the oil in the cotton cloth of her tights. *God*, how I wanted to flip over and see her pretty cunny revealed in the drenched, thin fabric!

I could hear Violet's breathing beginning to escalate and become raspy as she ground her pussy into my back, and I curled my fingers up to the sides of her thighs, caressing her with my hands. Recognizing that I was ready for some more direct engagement, she sat up and angled her knee against the side of my hip, signaling for me to turn over. With both of us now thoroughly coated in oil, I shifted my body and slowly flipped over, lingering for a moment at the sensation of my hips pressing into her gap while sliding over her dripping crotch.

Two can play this game of tantric teasing, I thought, smiling up at her.

But when I saw her magnificent tits for the first time with her large brown nipples, I lost any semblance of self-control, straining to lift my body to bring my face closer toward her. She smiled back at me and leaned forward to meet my face, and I sucked her teats hungrily into my mouth, engulfing them like a hungry calf feeding on her mother's udder. The oil had a pleasant citrus flavor, and I hummed happily that she'd been thoughtful enough to use edible oil, wondering if this was standard practice or if she'd simply taken my cues that I was ready for a different kind of engagement.

But with my face buried in her bosom and my hands squeezing her exquisite melons, it hardly mattered. For the next few minutes at least, I had her all to myself, and I was finally free to do as I pleased. Knowing that our time was soon going to run out, I reached down with my hands and pulled her ass higher up on my chest until she was straddling my face. When I saw the outline of her pussy through the transparent fabric of her tights, I tilted my head and began to suck on the wet cloth. But it was difficult for me to get traction on her clit with the barrier between us, even as she pressed her hips harder into my face while I nibbled on her the best I could with my teeth and stretched lips.

It felt glorious to be licking her pussy finally, but I was impatient to taste her directly and plunge my tongue into her dripping tunnel. Violet glanced up at the clock over the head of the table, then she lifted her legs and turned her body around, tilting her ass invitingly toward my head. When I saw her cotton-clad butt resting inches away from my face, I threaded my fingers under the waistband of her tights and began to pull them down over her hips. They bunched up near the top of her thighs, and she raised her hips over my head inviting me to pull them down all the way, and I practically ripped them off her body, throwing them onto the floor beneath us.

It looks like both of us will have some cleaning up to do after this, I smiled, staring at her glorious, naked butt for the first time.

Her skin was a beautiful chocolate brown color, but the folds of her vulva were bright pink, glistening with a mixture of scented oil and her own juices. I pulled her ass down hard onto my face and began gnawing on her like a wild animal with a bone. As much as I'd dreamt about slowly teasing and tormenting her the way she'd done with me, when I finally had the chance to ravish her, I couldn't resist the temptation to dive in head first.

When my lips encircled her pearl and my tongue slid over her nub, she pressed her pussy down harder onto my face, moaning softly. Exhilarated to finally have the chance to return the pleasure she'd given me, I began circling my hips unconsciously, and Violet lowered her head onto my own pussy, taking me into her mouth as we sucked on each other's clits, mashing our oily tits against one another's abdomens. The feeling of our warm bodies sliding over our joined skin was electric, and it didn't take long for the combination of erotic sensations to begin triggering the feeling of an oncoming climax.

But as our twisting and moaning began to escalate in pitch and volume, and I could feel myself nearing the point of no return, Violet suddenly lifted her head off my pussy and shifted her hips forward, away from my face. I tried to keep her from moving further away, but her heavily oiled skin didn't provide any traction, and she straightened her body up as she lifted her knees over my shoulders, sitting down over my chest. Desperate not to lose touch with her, I reached up with my hands, caressing the sides of her breasts while I rolled her nipples between my fingers.

She let me have my way with her for a few more seconds as she rolled her wet pussy all over my chest and tits, fucking each one of my breasts while she slid my rock-hard nipples between her dripping slit. Noticing my hips dry-humping the air over the massage table, she slowly inched her hips down the front of my stomach until she was straddling my bare mound. As she began to rock her hips over my hard pubis, she leaned forward, revealing her pretty bronze starfish for the first time.

Unable to resist the sight of it flexing and winking at me as she ground her cunt into my mound, I reached down with one hand and ran my thumb over her in the same way she'd done with me earlier. The sound of her grunting and moaning indicated that she was enjoying being touched there just as much as I did, and I was about to slip a finger in her hole when she pulled her body down a few inches lower, tantalizingly out of reach.

But when I felt the soft flesh of her folds at the base of her pubis meet my own, I tilted my hips forward and let out a long, guttural groan. The feeling of our pussies meeting for the first time was heavenly, and I strained to rock my hips under her weight in an effort to rub our clits together. But it was difficult for us to position our pussies in such a way for each of us to get the necessary friction we both desired, so Violet spread my knees further apart, kneeling on the padded table between me. Then she lifted my knees and pulled my legs back until I was in an upside-down squatted position.

With my dripping crease now perfectly positioned for her grinding pleasure, she spread her knees apart and crouched overtop of me, then lowered her pink vulva directly onto mine. When I felt her warm flesh melding against my own, I squealed in pleasure, flapping my hips against her. I felt a bit embarrassed humping her so impatiently, but I was mindful of the clock ticking behind us, and there was no way I was going to let her end this session without both of us achieving the height of pleasure.

Fortunately, she seemed just as committed to reaching climax before our time ended, and as the two of us slapped our bodies together moaning with increasing pleasure, I tilted my head up, watching her beautiful ass bobbing up and down over my gaping slit.

The sound and smell and feel of her magnificent body writhing against my own was a combination of sensations I couldn't resist any longer. As our moaning escalated toward our inevitable denouement, I turned my head toward the window and saw Violet peering back at me with her head tilted back in ecstasy and her mouth mawing open at the brink of ecstasy.

When our orgasms finally pounded over the two of us, we watched each other pitching and whining in mutual climax with the sparkling reflection of Lake Michigan shining upon us in supernatural splendor. When our orgasms finally began to subside after what seemed like an eternity, Violet leaned forward resting her torso on the base of the massage table between my legs while I peered down watching the juices dribbling out of her pretty flower onto our connected mounds.

I glanced up at the clock over my head and smiled, noticing that we'd gone a full fifteen minutes over our allotted time. Something told me this final session in my allotted massage package wouldn't be the last time the two of us had a chance to explore a transcendent level of enlightened pleasure.

THE HAREM

A STEAMY ADVENTURE

1

___

As I walked through the open-air market in Marrakesh, I could feel my heart pounding in my chest. I'd never been to Morocco before, and the hustle and bustle of the *Souk Semmarine* was a feast for the senses. With so many tourists and locals crammed into the narrow laneways, my eyes darted from one distraction to another. While I strolled past their stalls, shopkeepers noisily hawked their wares, begging me to make an offer on everything from cheap jewelry to handbags. The pungent aroma of grilled kebabs, fresh hummus, and fried snails permeated my nose. Everywhere I looked, women in long, full-body burkas or face-concealing niqabs passed calmly by, seemingly unperturbed by the chaos of the teeming bazaar. With my long blonde hair and tight jeans, I definitely stood out like a sore thumb in this conservative muslim metropolis.

After a half hour or so, I grew tired of the peddlers confronting me, and I ducked into one of the shops to try on some head scarves, hoping to distract attention from my obvious Western appearance. When I tried a pretty pink and teal colored one on and looked at myself in the tiny mirror on the wall, the owner came up behind me, smiling at my reflection.

"Very pretty," he said. "You like?"

"Maybe," I said, mindful of the hard-sell personality of local merchants that I'd been forewarned about. "How much is it?"

"For you, pretty lady, only five hundred dirham!"

Knowing the local exchange rate was roughly ten dirham for one U.S. dollar, fifty bucks for a scarf didn't seem out of line. But I also knew that shop owners in North African bazaars were notorious for fleecing unaware tourists and that haggling was an expected and necessary condition of purchase.

"That's more than I can afford," I said, placing the garment back on the rack.

"Perhaps we can make an accommodation," he said, lifting the scarf off the shelf and placing it back on my head. "Since the colors match your eyes so perfectly."

"Um-hmm," I smiled, knowing full well he was just buttering me up for a sale.

"How about two-fifty?" I said, placing my hands on my hips defiantly.

"Ps-shaw!" the merchant scoffed. "That is well below my cost. This is an authentic Moroccan hijab. Other merchants sell this style for much more."

"Well, I guess I'll just have to go check *them* out then," I said, placing the scarf in his hands and turning to exit the stall.

"Ok, ok!" he backpedaled, catching up with me and blocking my exit. "New price, only for you. Four-fifty. But that's as low as I can go."

"That's not much of a discount," I huffed. "Other vendors have offered far better. Three hundred is the best I can do."

The man threw up his hands, wrinkling his brow with a sad puppy dog face.

"My lady, I wish I could help you, but I'm just a poor merchant with high overhead. Don't you expect me to make a profit?"

"Of course," I said. "But I know most of these items have a high markup. I think you've still got plenty of profit to work with here. Perhaps I'll come back after comparing prices with some of the other sellers."

"Wait, wait," the man said, stepping in front of me again. "I can't have you leave without purchasing something. Four hundred is my best offer. But at that price, you're practically *stealing* it from me."

I picked up the scarf again, turning it over to look for some kind of label.

"How do I know this is even made here? There's no tag."

"Oh please," the man said, crossing his arms. "Now you *insult* me. We only sell authentic textiles manufactured in this country. Look at the intricate stitching. This is hand-embroidered right here in Morocco."

"And the fabric?" I said, rolling the cloth between my fingers. "Is it genuine silk?"

The man placed the garment under an overhead ceiling light, slowly tilting it from side to side.

"Can't you see how the patina changes color when you bend the fabric? I would never sell cheap polyester at my store. This is where all the local muslim women come to purchase authentic Arab clothing."

"Okay," I said, shaking my head in surrender. "I'll offer a little more since I can tell it's a quality product. "I will pay three hundred and fifty dirham, cash. That is all I have on my person."

The merchant paused for a moment, scanning my face with a stern expression as if trying to divine my thoughts. Then he burst into a broad smile, nodding enthusiastically.

"Only for you, my pretty American," he said. "And only because I don't want to see you walking around the bazaar in a cheap knock-off sold by the other vendors."

"Good," I said, turning back toward the mirror. "Do you mind showing me the proper way to wear it? The way the local women do?"

"Of course," he said, draping the scarf over the top of my head and pulling the ends softly under my chin, tying them in a gentle knot. "The idea is to cover your hair and tie it so it covers as much of your face as possible. Our culture requires women to express their modesty by covering their bodies when they are out in public."

"Thank you," I said, pulling some bills out of my pocket and handing him the agreed-upon amount.

"Please, come again," the man said, bowing with his palms centered over his chest. "I have many more items of clothing that you would look beautiful in."

"I'll try to come back before I leave your beautiful country," I nodded. "Thank you for your time."

"Safe travels," he said, waving goodbye to me as I exited the stall.

While I continued down the main thoroughfare jostled by distracted tourists, aggressive shopkeepers, and beguiling snake charmers, I realized the thin head covering provided limited camouflage from my fair skin and Western clothing. By the time I exited the packed marketplace, I was visibly sweating and exhausted. I found a nearby cafe and ordered a strong coffee, then found a vacant table in the corner and sat down, nursing my drink.

Most of the patrons appeared to be Westerners, but on the far side of the room sat a lone man in long white robes wearing a traditional headdress, sipping a beverage. I'd always been fascinated by the clothing and customs of native Arabs, and as he appraised the boisterous tourists gathering in the cafe, he peered at them bemused. The man had dark, weathered skin and a closely cropped beard with soft brown eyes and a square jawline. Appearing to be in his late thirties or early forties, he was quite handsome, with the juxtaposition of his flowing cream-colored kaftan and his golden-brown skin making him look like a young Omar Sharif.

As he casually glanced around the cafe, he caught me staring at him, and I quickly looked away. Moments later, my gaze was drawn back to him and this time he smiled when our eyes met. When I looked away again, he stood up from his table and went to the front counter where he placed an order for something. A few minutes later, the clerk handed him two steaming cups and the man began walking in my direction.

"Excuse me," he said, approaching my table. "I noticed you were sitting alone and wondered if you'd like some company. I brought you a cup of mint tea if you'd like to sample some of our local fare."

"Um..." I hesitated, looking around the room to make sure it was safe to be seen in the company of a stranger.

Normally, I'd quickly rebuff someone who made such a bold and unsolicited advance, but there was something about his quiet demeanor and warm eyes that put me at ease.

"Thank you," I said, shifting my chair back a few inches. "That would be lovely."

"My name's Amir," he said, handing me the cup of steaming tea.

"Jade," I said, nodding politely toward him.

"That's a lovely name. It sounds Asian or Moorish, but you look much *fairer* than that."

"Yes," I laughed. "I suppose my light skin gives me away. I'm from Chicago actually, in the United States."

"I know it well," he nodded. "The Sears Tower, Navy Pier, Millennium Park..."

"You've *been* to the United States?" I said, surprised by his fluent English and knowledge of my local landmarks.

"I spent four years studying law at Columbia University and traveled throughout the country during my summers off."

"I *wondered* where your perfect English came from," I said, smiling at his handsome face. "I never would have guessed–"

"That a sheep-herder like me might be so worldly?" he joked.

"No," I stammered. "I meant–"

"It's okay," he laughed. "It's a common reaction I get from Westerners. They either expect me to be some kind of sultan or a terrorist wearing these clothes."

"I'd never judge a person simply on the basis of what they're wearing," I said, furrowing my brow in sympathy.

"That's very wise," he said, peering up at my scarf. "What about you? You seem to be a little more...*restrained* compared to your fellow countrymen."

I lifted my hand self-consciously to my scarf and chuckled.

"I felt a little exposed walking around the markets with my long blonde hair. I think I was too easy a mark for your local merchants."

The man took a sip of his tea and chuckled.

"They can be a little overbearing at times when it comes to

approaching tourists. There's something to be said for exercising a little decorum and good manners."

"I couldn't agree more," I said, lifting my cup in agreement.

"So, what brings you so far from home?"

"Just looking for a change of pace, I guess. I've never been to this part of the world and I wanted to experience the unique culture of North Africa."

"Where have you been so far?"

"Just the medina and a few of the museums. But I'd love to see more of the countryside."

"You mean the *desert*? There's really only two climate zones in the Mediterranean crescent–the fertile orchards near the sea and the barren plains of the Sahara."

"I guess I'm more drawn to the desert. Maybe it's from watching all those romantic films like Lawrence of Arabia and The Wind and the Lion. There's something about the natural beauty of the red sand and the windswept dunes that seems so peaceful and alluring. It seems to be about as far away from the hustle and bustle of the urban jungle as you could possibly get."

"Have you ever ridden a camel?"

"It's on my bucket list."

"Would you like to join my caravan for a little excursion?"

"Caravan?" I said, widening my eyes. "You're traveling in a *caravan*?"

"Yes," he nodded. "It's a modest group. A few camels, some livestock, and my small coterie."

"Is that how you get around?" I asked, suddenly intrigued by this mysterious stranger. "Where are you from originally?"

"I was born in Jordan, but I come from a Bedouin family. We're nomads, moving from country to country, buying and selling livestock and living off the land."

"So you really are a–"

"Goat herder?" he laughed. "In a manner of speaking. But as the leader of my tribe, I'm officially considered a *sheikh*."

"But what about Columbia...?"

"My wealthy parents sent me there hoping for bigger things for me. But I prefer this simple life. There's something to be said for the freedom and stress-free life of a traveling vagabond. I get to meet interesting people in all the countries along the North African peninsula."

"Just like Sean Connery in the movie The Wind and the Lion," I smiled.

"I suppose, insofar as being the king of my domain and living a nomadic lifestyle. So what do you say? Do you feel as brave as Candice Bergen?"

"As I recall, she didn't exactly go *willingly* into the Sahara wilderness with her would-be captor. And I don't have any romantic intentions..."

"No worries," the man said. "You can stay as long or as short as you prefer, or even just for a day trip through the edge of the desert on one of my camels. I assure you that I have plenty of *other* distractions at my disposal."

I pinched my eyebrows, appraising the mysterious man in luxurious robes. I had no doubt that he had little trouble attracting beautiful women wherever he traveled.

"How would this work exactly?" I said, crossing my arms. "I've never run off with a strange man into the desert before."

"I understand your hesitation," he said. "My camp is just outside the city limits. You can join my troupe for an authentic Bedouin dinner while you stay with my other wives in a separate tent. If you feel so-inclined, you're free to join us on the next leg of our journey toward Algiers. I'll be happy to pay for your safe passage back to Morocco if that's where you've made return travel arrangements."

I paused for a moment, scanning his face for any sign of ill intent. I'd heard about the legal practice of polygamy in certain Arab countries, and far from turning me off, the idea of being surrounded by other women who could satisfy his sexual needs gave me a certain degree of comfort.

"That won't be necessary," I said. "It shouldn't be too difficult to change my airfare if necessary. But how can I be sure you don't intend to steal me away like Sean Connery and add me to your stable of harem girls?"

"That's not the way we operate," he laughed. "As you probably learned from watching that movie. Honor is the most important character trait among we Bedouin. But of course, I would encourage you to leave a message with your friends and family before you leave."

The man took a menu scrap from the table and scribbled something on the paper.

"This is my full name. I'm well known in most towns along the coast. The last thing I need is the American cavalry hunting me down like in the movie. I assure you, this is an honorable offer between friends. You have my word on that."

"Can you give me a day to think it over?" I asked, still not convinced this was a good idea. But the lure of joining a real caravan through the Sahara Desert was awfully tempting.

"Absolutely," Amir said. "If you decide to join me, let's meet in this cafe at the same time tomorrow. If you're not here, I'll understand and there will be no hard feelings. But if you do decide to come, we can take a taxi to the outskirts of the city where my aide will meet us and escort us by camel to my camp at the edge of the desert."

"How will I keep from falling off?" I smiled.

"It's not as scary as it looks to ride a camel," he said. "There are comfortable and secure saddles, and they walk quite slowly. But if you're still worried, you can always ride tandem with me."

"I'm sure I'll be fine," I smiled, turning my wrist to check the time. "Thank you for your kind offer, Amir. I look forward to meeting you again tomorrow at five p.m. And thank you for the tea."

As I rose to leave, he stood along with me, extending his hand.

"I hope to see you again, lovely Jade," he said, clasping my hand softly. "And keep an eye out for those carnival barkers. Best to keep your hijab on while you're walking about town."

"Will do," I said, heading toward the exit door.

After I left the cafe, I closed my eyes, inhaling the warm arid air of the Moroccan town square. Something told me that my North African adventure was about to take an interesting new turn.

2

───────────

For the next twenty-four hours, I vacillated back and forth on whether to entertain the handsome sheikh's offer. On the one hand, I'd always dreamed about trekking through the Sahara Desert on a camel. But I knew that traveling into the wilderness with a total stranger was not without its risks. He could easily abduct or molest me, with no guarantee that the local police would make any effort to find me or hold him to account. I knew that muslim law was highly skewed in favor of the man's rights and that women were often ostracized or worse for any kind of perceived sexual indiscretion.

The following morning after enjoying a light breakfast, I approached the front desk of my riad to enquire about the mysterious man. If he was as important and well-traveled as he claimed to be, I figured the staff of one of the best hotels in Marrakesh would have heard of him. But if he was an unknown or persona non grata, I'd simply ignore his invitation and remain in the relative safety of the downtown tourist areas.

"Excuse me," I said, slipping Amir's handwritten note across the counter towards the attending clerk. "Can you tell me if you've heard of this man?"

The clerk squinted at the writing then looked up at me and smiled.

"Of course," he said. "Mr. Haddad is one of our frequent guests. Would you like me to see if he's staying at the hotel?"

"Um, no, thank you," I said. "It's just that he invited me to take a tour with his caravan and I wondered if this was, you know–*safe* or irregular."

"I can't vouch for how often he entertains Westerners in his cavalcade, but he is often seen in the company of attractive young women such as yourself, and I've never heard of any complaints or misconduct. The Sheikh is widely respected as a man of honor and prestige in these parts. I'm quite sure that you would not only be safe, but indeed well-protected while under his guardianship."

"Thank you," I said, placing the note back in my pocket.

As the hour approached for our planned reconnection, I packed a light duffel bag of overnight clothes and sent an email to my best friend Hannah from back home.

Han,

Enjoying my trip to Morocco so far. Will send more pics soon. I've accepted an invitation to go on a private caravan tour of the local desert with a prominent bedouin leader. His name is Amir Haddad. Apparently his family is quite prominent in Jordan.

If you don't hear back from me in a few days, contact the local embassy to see if they can track my whereabouts. I know this sounds crazy, but I've always dreamed of traveling the Sahara on camelback, and you only live once!

Talk soon,

Jade

I knotted my silk scarf under my chin, then placed a wide-brimmed straw hat on my head and headed back towards the cafe where I'd met the sheikh the previous day. With my heart beating a million miles an hour, I strolled past the bustling souks wondering what I'd gotten myself into.

W hen I entered the cafe and saw Amir sitting in the corner with his legs crossed sipping a cup of tea, he smiled and stood as I approached his table.

"I'm glad you decided to join me again, Jade," he said, holding out his hand as he supported me while I lowered myself onto the adjoining chair. "I was afraid that I might have scared you away with my rather direct proposition."

"I went back and forth considering it, to be honest," I said. "But I asked around, and you were truthful about your reputation. Apparently, I'm not the *first* tourist you've entertained in this manner. But I left your credentials with the U.S. Embassy just in case."

"I would expect no less from such a wise and pretty lady," he smiled. "May I order you a cup of tea?"

I looked at my watch and glanced outside at the lengthening afternoon shadows.

"I'm already pretty charged up about this adventure," I said, concerned about traveling at night deep into the outback. "Shouldn't we head out to your camp while there's still good light?"

"As you wish," he said, standing up and extending his hand as he surveyed my wardrobe. "I see you've come well prepared for the elements. Though I'm not sure about that hat. You look more like *Audrey Hepburn* in Breakfast at Tiffany's than Candice Bergen in The Wind and the Lion."

I smiled at his genteel manners while he opened the cafe exit door for me then hailed a passing taxi. After we got in the cab and he gave the driver directions in arabic, he glanced down at my overnight bag.

"It looks like you're intending to stay for a while," he smiled. "I must not have scared you *too* much with my abrupt proposition."

"I've heard it's a pretty big desert," I said, pulling my handbag closer toward me. Unbeknownst to my host, I'd included a can of pepper spray under my belongings in case he got the wrong idea. "A girl can never be too prepared on these kinds of expeditions."

"Indeed it is," he smiled. "Did you know that the entirety of the Sahara Desert is even bigger than the continental United States? But never fear–my caravan has enough provisions to keep us comfortable for as long as you choose to stay."

As the taxi sped towards the outskirts of the city, I watched the passing scenery as it became progressively less populated and more barren. Within twenty minutes, the dusty streets soon gave way to grassy hillsides. When we crested the final ridge and I saw the open expanse of the desert stretching out in every direction, I gasped. The late afternoon sun cast long shadows over the undulating red sand dunes, making it look like a different *planet*.

"Is this your first time seeing the desert?" Amir asked, noticing my wide eyes surveying the eerie landscape.

"First time up close and for *real*," I nodded in a daze. "It's even more magnificent than I imagined."

"It has a way of transporting you," he nodded. "There's something about the open vistas and the way the sun reflects over the shifting sands that's quite captivating. Perhaps now you can begin to appreciate how I'm are attracted by its allure."

"It *is* mesmerizing, I grant you," I said. "But how do you navigate your way across this moonscape? There are no roads or landmarks to know which way you're headed?"

"We navigate by the shadows of the sun during the day and the stars in the evening. Plus, the desert isn't all sand. There are bluffs and oases and mountain ridges that point our way. We bedouin have traveled the deserts of North Africa for thousands of years. We know it as well as the back of our hands, as you Americans say."

"I'll have to take your word for it," I said, suddenly feeling the dryness in my mouth. "But something tells me I should have packed more bottles of water in my overnight case. How far away is your camp?"

"It's only twenty or thirty minutes by camel ride," Amir said as the taxi skidded to a stop at the end of the road. Nestled in a shaded dale of the hillside, I noticed a dark-skinned Arab man in a long tunic tending to three camels. "My aide brought an extra ride for you. Don't worry about the water. We've long-since learned how to manage our scarce resources in the parched desert."

Amir paid the taxi driver then escorted me to the dale where he introduced me to his servant.

"This is Ali," Amir said, motioning toward the other man. "He'll look after all of your needs during your stay with us."

The man bowed slightly at the waist, acknowledging me as Amir's guest. I found it a bit strange that Amir didn't introduce me by name, but I assumed it had something to do with the customs of his tribe and his status as leader of the clan.

I glanced at the three oddly shaped animals nibbling on grass besides us. With their long knobby legs, U-shaped neck, and large hump in the middle of their back, they looked like a cross between a llama and an oversized donkey. Towering at least two feet over the top of my head, I was already starting to get vertigo imagining myself trying to balance on top of their precarious mounds.

"These are a lot *taller* than I imagined," I said, noticing an absence of stirrups hanging from their woven cloth saddles. "How will I ever get on top of it?"

"You don't climb up on a camel like you would a horse," Amir said. "They kneel down for you to get on top of them."

He mentioned something to his aide in arabic and Ali pulled on the long hair on the side of one of the camels, then the animal knelt down on the ground with its front knees and lowered its back end until its belly was lying flat on the ground.

"Wow," I said. "That's certainly convenient. Have you trained them this way only for your guests, or is this the way *everybody* mounts a camel?"

"They're very domesticated," Amir said. "It's easy enough to climb atop a standing camel if you know how, but this certainly makes it a lot easier."

"I'll say," I nodded, seeing the top of the cloth saddle now resting at hip height.

"But you still need to be careful to hold on to the pommel at the front of the camel's saddle to make sure you don't get bucked off when it stands. It jerks forward and back as it rises, and if you're not used to it, you can easily be thrown."

Amir said something to Ali and he held out his hand, motioning for me to climb atop the saddle of the resting camel, and I swung my leg up over his hump and sat down on the surprisingly comfortable seat. Although the frame appeared to be made entirely of wood, I noticed a padding of straw and palm leaves under the thick woven blankets draped over its flanks.

"Okay," Amir said. "Now grasp the knob on the front of the saddle tightly and clamp your legs against the side of the camel as he rises."

I did as Amir instructed, then Ali tapped the side of the animal and it lurched forward lifting its back end, then it stepped forward with both front legs until it was fully erect. My body swung wildly as it see-sawed up to a standing position, and I could feel my heart beating as I stared down at the ground ten feet below me.

"Are you good?" Amir called up to me, seeing the fright in my eyes.

"Yes, as long as I don't fall off," I grunted. "But how do I *steer* this thing?"

"Don't worry about that," he laughed. "Ali will lead your camel with a tether behind his animal. But watch out as he begins to walk. They have a bit of a jerky gait. Try to relax your body and let it sway with the animal's movements. Are you ready to head out to our camp?"

I nodded my head then Amir and Ali mounted their camels, heading out in a straight line toward the open desert with Amir in the lead. It didn't take long for me to get used to my camel's rhythmic up-and-down gait, and as I began to relax, I looked out over the vast expanse of russet-colored dunes at the exquisite beauty of the desert. Looking like a giant Rothko painting, all I could see was an endless sea of golden waves juxtaposed against the brilliant blue sky.

The air was hot and dry, and I blinked as sprinkles of sand dusted up into my eyes from the strong wind sweeping across the dunes. More than once I had to grab my hat from falling off my head from the gusts shooting overtop the crescent-shaped hillocks. As I watched the long shadows of our three camels traipse across the soft turf, I smiled at the serene beauty and solitude of the glittering landscape. I wasn't sure what awaited me at Amir's camp, but for the time being, the gentle loping of my camel and the whisper of the warm Saharan breeze lulled me into a blissful, trancelike state.

3

____

Thirty minutes later, I noticed a clump of trees on the horizon, and I squinted through the shimmering haze wondering if it was a mirage. But as we got closer, I saw a small collection of tents nestled among the palms and a flock of livestock grazing on the grass surrounding the perimeter of the encampment. Hardly believing my eyes, I called ahead to Amir, wondering how anything could grow in this barren wasteland.

"Is this your camp?" I shouted over the howling wind.

"Yes," he said, pulling his camel up beside mine so I could hear him better.

"I thought my eyes were playing tricks on me at first," I said, shaking my head in astonishment. "How does any vegetation survive out here without any water?"

"The desert is riddled with a labyrinth of underground aquifers," he said. "In certain places, natural springs bring the water to the surface, feeding the surrounding vegetation. At other oases, manmade wells tap the aquifers, supplying much needed water to traveling caravans such as my own."

"I thought oases were just a figment of Western movies. I had no idea they actually existed in the middle of the desert."

"There are actually quite a few scattered across the Sahara," he nodded. "But because of the vast size of the desert, it can take many days on camel to travel between them. They've been the lifeblood of we bedouin for centuries."

As we got closer to the camp, I noticed a large herd of camels and scores of sheep and goats grazing quietly in the grass.

"And there's enough water to feed all those *animals* too?"

"Yes," Amir said. "The aquifers are practically endless. There's a veritable ocean of water underneath this arid surface. Did you know that the Sahara was once an enormous sea before the Earth's shifting plates separated the large continents of Eurasia and Africa?"

"I had no idea," I said, growing increasingly impressed with Amir's knowledge of world history and geology. "But why do you have so many camels and livestock? You must have quite a large entourage."

"Actually, it's mostly just me and Ali and my stable of wives. The animals are primarily used to transport our gear and provide food for our band."

"Wow, you really *are* a self-contained entity out here in the middle of the wilderness, aren't you?"

"Everything we need is supplied by the animals and the desert," he nodded.

"And your *wives*," I smiled, peering ahead toward Ali plodding along in front of us, wondering how he satisfied some of *his* more primal needs.

"Yes," Amir smiled. "And my wives."

When we reached the edge of the trees, I noticed a group of women kneeling in the sand preparing food. They all wore loose-fitting tunics and cotton headdresses that wrapped tightly around their heads and faces, providing protection from the overhead sun and the dusty wind. As our retinue approached the center of the camp, the women looked up and stared at me like I was from another planet. They all seemed young and strikingly beautiful.

Maybe Amir doesn't need to entertain Western women after all, I thought.

The two men dismounted their camels, then Amir tapped my

animal and he knelt onto the ground, where Amir offered his hand to help me dismount. Then he led me into one of the two large tents in the campground where an attractive dark-haired woman roughly my age was folding clothes in the corner of the enclosure.

"This is my wife, Laila," he said, introducing me to the woman. "Laila, Jade will be joining us for dinner this evening, so please make sure she has everything she needs."

She turned around and smiled at me with her piercing eyes. I was surprised how beautiful she looked bereft of any makeup or other embellishments. Her wraparound headdress framed her pretty face, highlighting her high cheekbones and golden-brown skin.

"Pleased to meet you," Laila said, bowing slightly at the waist.

It was hard to discern her figure under her layered cloak, but my pussy fluttered when I saw her face flush slightly in modesty.

"You speak *English*?" I said, surprised by her absence of any discernible accent.

"Yes," she said. "My family is from Cairo and we learned English in elementary school. I'm a bit rusty, so it will be nice to have a native speaker to help me brush up on my skills."

"We'll be having dinner when the sun goes down," Amir interrupted. "Then I'll be providing some special entertainment in my tent later on. You may wish to put on some warmer clothes, as it can get quite chilly outside after dark. I'll see you in another hour or so."

After Amir exited the tent, I peered at Laila with a quizzical look. "*Entertainment?*"

"Never fear," she chuckled. "He often entertains visitors with a traditional arab dance. Though it's usually for the benefit of other men. This is the first time he's brought a Western *woman* into his camp."

"I guess I should be honored then," I shrugged, wondering exactly what kind of dance he had in mind.

Laila peered at my cut-off capri pants and light linen blouse and smiled.

"Would you like to change into something more comfortable? As

Amir said, it gets quite cold at night and you'll want a bit more protection against the blowing wind."

"Sure," I said, happy to adopt the local customs during my brief visit with the group.

"If you'd like to remove your clothing, I can store them in a safe location while you stay with us."

"*Everything*?" I said, wondering what arab men and women wore underneath their long garments.

"It's more comfortable that way," she said. "Unless you need to wear something because it's that time of the month...?"

"No, thankfully," I chuckled, curious how they also managed *that* aspect of their personal hygiene.

As I began to remove my clothing, Laila peered at me, noticing the strange tan lines around my bra and upper arms. I paused for a moment before pulling off my panties, and her eyes widened when she saw my shaved pubis. I felt like a bit of a freak, realizing that she and the rest of the women rarely went outside with any exposed skin and almost certainly abstained from any kind of intimate grooming.

Laila fetched a neatly folded garment from the corner of the tent then opened it up to reveal an ankle-length tunic with long sleeves and an opening at the top. I held up my arms and she draped it over my body, stepping in close to me as she peered into my eyes. She smelled of jasmine and lemongrass, and my heart fluttered as her full lips neared my mouth when the garment fell over my shoulders. Then she wrapped a long cotton scarf over my head and under my chin, fastening it with a bobby pin at the ends to hold it in place.

I guess they're not completely bereft of Western conveniences, I smiled.

When she finished, she stepped back and nodded approvingly, smiling at the unusual appearance of a Western woman dressed in traditional arabian garb.

"Do you have a mirror or something to view myself in?" I asked, intrigued to see what I looked like.

"I'm afraid we don't," she said. "It is not part of our culture for women to primp over their external appearance. But I assure you that you look quite beautiful."

"Thank you," I said, reaching into my bag to retrieve my phone. I tapped the screen a few times then handed the device to Laila. "I know this must sound terribly touristy of me, but would you mind taking a picture of me? My friends back home will never believe that I got myself into this arrangement, and I'd love to have a keepsake of my visit to your camp."

"Okay," Laila said, squinting her eyes at the phone. "But this is a little different from the phones I remember using in my youth. How does it work?"

"Just step back and angle the phone until you see my entire body on the screen, then tap the red button at the bottom to capture the image."

Laila did as I requested and I heard the familiar shutter sound when the phone took the picture. She handed it back to me and I tapped the thumbnail image in the lower corner of the screen to view the full-size image. I laughed when I saw myself encased in the flowing robes, with only my pale face peering through the wrap-around fabric.

"That's certainly a different look for me," I said, feeling the soft fabric brushing against my hardening nipples and bare mound. "But I have to admit, it's a lot more comfortable than my usual attire. Is it comfortable to wear in the heat of the day?"

Laila pulled the fabric up over my shoulders and I felt a puff of air press up from the floor toward my exposed pussy.

"The cotton fabric breathes nicely, and the loose fit permits the wind to flow over our bare bodies underneath," Laila smiled.

"Yes, I can see that," I said. "I'm *already* beginning to appreciate the extra freedom of movement in this dress. Although I don't imagine you call it that in your native language."

"We women refer to it as a *thawb*, but when men wear similar robes, they call it a kaftan."

I nodded, beginning to understand the various ways arab culture subjugated women under the control of men. I crossed my arms, beginning to feel the chill as the sun began to set over the horizon.

"Do you think this will this be warm enough in the evening?"

Laila pulled a wool blanket off the pile of clothes in the corner and placed it over my shoulders.

"This shawl will help keep you warm," she smiled. "And it can also be used as a bed covering later on at night."

"Speaking of," I said. "I see you don't have any traditional beds in the tent..."

"We bedouin can't afford such luxuries," Laila laughed. "Everything has to be light enough to pack onto the backs of our camels when we move from one location to the next. We sleep on woven blankets on the soft sand. I think you'll find it's quite comfortable, actually."

"Does everyone sleep in this one tent?" I said, peering at the limited amount of floor space in the twenty-by-twenty-foot enclosure.

"All of the *women*, yes," Laila nodded. "The men have separate tents, of course. Everything is tightly controlled in our caravan. Nothing goes to waste."

"So I'm beginning to learn," I smiled, imagining myself lying on the soft desert sand next to the covey of beautiful women at night.

"Are you hungry?" she asked.

The mention of food made my stomach grumble. I suddenly realized that I hadn't eaten since early in the morning.

"Oh yes, very."

"Come, let's show you how we prepare our traditional bedouin meals."

Laila led me outside, where a large open fire cackled in a sand pit with a wooden frame erected overtop of its perimeter. The women sat in a large circle around the flame, hunched over in their long robes, kneading their hands into large porcelain bowls.

"It smells heavenly," I said, breathing in the fresh scent of milk and spices. "May I ask what the women are preparing?"

"It's a rice dish infused with fresh goat milk, lentils, and chopped onions, seasoned with saffron and turmeric."

"So you're all *vegetarians*?"

"Oh no," Laila said. "We also eat goat meat and lamb. But that's usually reserved for special occasions, like when we have a guest such as yourself."

"I see," I said, noticing Amir flipping open the canvas door of his tent and walking in our direction.

"I see that Laila has gotten you into some more comfortable clothes," he nodded approvingly. "Are you ready to enjoy our traditional bedouin dinner?"

"Absolutely," I said. "I don't know if it's this desert heat or the long camel ride, but I'm famished!"

"Well, we won't delay any longer then," he said, brandishing a curved knife from under his kaftan. He walked up to one of the younger sheep grazing quietly at the edge of the pasture and he grabbed the animal by the back of its head, calmly slicing its throat. The lamb staggered for a moment in shock, then fell to the ground twitching its legs for a few seconds, then lay still as the blood from its neck coated the desert sand. Seconds later, Ali approached the dead animal, and using a longer knife proceeded to slice open its belly, pulling out its entrails.

"Oh my God," I dry-heaved, turning away from the scene of the gory slaughter.

"You've never seen a live animal killed before?" Amir said, seeing my discomfort.

"Never up close and in person like this," I coughed, trying to keep myself from retching.

"But you eat meat?"

"Yes, it's just that–"

"You Westerners are insulated by your supermarkets and hidden slaughterhouses from the act of killing and preparing the animal."

"Yes," I said, realizing how hypocritical it was of me to be offended by the practice of killing live animals for consumption.

"A halal slaughter is considered the most humane way of killing an animal in our culture," he said. "The animal hardly feels a thing before it loses consciousness and quickly bleeds out."

"I'll take your word for it," I said, watching Ali skin the animal and thread a stake through its mouth as he placed it over the fire pit.

"I hope this won't diminish your appetite for the meal. Everything should be ready in another half hour or so."

"I'm sure I'll be fine," I said, smelling the scent of the fresh meat cooking over the pit. "I just need a moment to collect myself."

"Come join me then by the fire while the women make the final preparations."

Amir motioned to a blanket spread out on the sand about ten feet away from the fire, and he held my hand while I sat down on the mat.

"So, what do you think of our little caravan so far?" he said, sitting down cross-legged beside me.

"It's certainly *authentic*," I said, peering at the group of young women preparing the dishes in the circle around the fire. "But I'm wondering about the ratio of men to women in your troupe. Are all of these women your wives?"

"Not in the *legal* sense," he said. "I prefer to think of them as my courtesans."

"They're all so young and pretty. How did they come to join your caravan?"

"I bought them," Amir said nonchalantly.

"You *what*?"

"I know this is a custom frowned upon in the West. But it is quite common in conservative muslim cultures, especially among we bedouin. Families consider it an honor for their daughters to be indentured to a prominent sheikh such as myself."

"And when they get *older*? Do you simply dispose of them when they no longer suit your fancy?"

"They're sold off to other prominent men as maids, nannies, and cooks. The women are always treated well, generally enjoying lives far more comfortable and secure than in their own impoverished families."

"And in the meantime, they travel in your caravan for your own amusement?"

"Well, as you can see, they perform many *other* useful functions. Nobody goes for want in my troupe. Everyone's needs are fully satisfied."

"What about *Ali's* needs?" I said, noticing his servant dutifully turning the roast lamb on the fire spit. "Does he also enjoy the company of these attractive ladies?"

"He would never dare *touch* one of my women for fear of instant execution," Amir said, suddenly clenching his jaw. "But he's well compensated for his service to the caravan. He satisfies his more primal needs in the many small towns along our route."

"I see," I said, watching him remove the charred carcass from the spit then carving it up into smaller chunks and passing them around the circle. Each of the women took a piece and sliced it up into bite-sized portions, mixing them in with their bowls of rice.

"Come," Amir said, taking two bowls and placing them in front of us. "Let's not be concerned about such indelicate matters over dinner. Let's enjoy our feast under the stars of this magnificent canopy."

He picked up his bowl and dipped his hand into the dish, pinching skewers of meat and rice between his fingers and bringing it to his mouth. Looking around the circle, I saw the rest of the entourage doing the same, and I picked up my bowl not wanting to be rude, following their lead. The food was surprisingly moist and tender, with the milk-infused rice keeping all the ingredients bound together, making it easier to take bite-sized chunks in my fingers. I hummed appreciatively at the piquant taste of the freshly prepared ingredients, soon forgetting about the unsettling scene that I'd witnessed with the young lamb moments before.

As we all ate quietly around the circle, my eyes scanned the faces of the pretty young women peering at me curiously across the dancing flames of the bonfire. It didn't take long for my mind to wander to what *other* forms of entertainment they used to keep themselves amused when Amir was otherwise occupied. Surely, he couldn't keep *all* of them satisfied at one time, I thought. As my pussy twitched from the cool desert breeze wafting up under my fluttering robe, I began to look forward to sleeping on the soft desert sand later in the evening.

4

———————

After dinner, Amir invited Laila and me to his tent to enjoy the planned entertainment. He motioned for two of the girls to prepare for the event, and they left the circle while the rest of the women cleaned up the dishes. When I entered his enclosure, I was surprised at how large it was for one person. More than twice the size of the women's shelter, it was bedecked with persian rugs, beautiful tapestries, and a large wood-frame bed with luxury linens.

Wow, I thought, shaking my head in dismay. *Arab men really do enjoy all the advantages in this culture.*

Amir invited the two of us to sit on the plush carpet in the center of the tent, then he fetched a heart-shaped guitar from the corner and sat down between us with the instrument cradled between his legs. A few moments later, I heard two women's voices outside the front door of his tent and Amir replied to them in arabic. When they pulled back the flap and entered the room, my eyes flew open in shock. Instead of their usual long robes and wraparound headdresses, they wore a skimpy ornamental bikini costume.

Their long black hair was held in place by a beaded headband with long tassels hanging down over their eyes, festooned with little silver bells. Dangling from their tasseled bikini bottom hung a knee-length black cloth that provided a modicum of modesty to cover their crotch area. But the rest of the costume left little to the imagination, showing the deep cleavage between their tightly compressed breasts and their exposed bellies and thighs glistening in the soft candlelight of Amir's tent.

Shifting from the ultra-conservative full-body covering of their traditional frocks to this bawdy costume was a shock to my system, and I soaked up the women's taut, sexy figures like I hadn't seen a near-naked body in weeks. Which I damn near *hadn't*. Suddenly realizing that I hadn't felt the touch of another woman's body since I left home, my pussy throbbed while I ogled the sexy girls standing only a few feet in front of me.

"Are you ready to watch a real arabian belly dance?" Amir said, noticing my pupils dilated in excitement.

"Definitely," I smiled, eager to see the two women gyrate their bodies next to me.

He nodded toward the two girls and they stepped back a few feet, then he picked up the guitar and began strumming a rhythmic folk tune. As the melody filled the cabin, the two women began to undulate their hips in unison, matching the beat of the song. My eyes flickered over their bodies, absorbing the sensuous spectacle while their stomach muscles flexed and their navels swayed from side to side like two winking eyes. As they stepped forward and back in perfect harmony, they snapped the castanets on the tips of their fingers together, providing a rhythmic accompaniment to Amir's lilting melody.

Just when I thought this guy couldn't get any more suave and sophisticated, I thought. *He even plays the guitar perfectly.*

In another place and time, I might have fallen for his seductive demeanor, but for the time being I was utterly hypnotized by the sensual moves of the two beautiful women dancing before me. As I watched their eyes gazing at us behind their swinging ringlets, I tried to place how old they were. Their bodies hardly had an ounce of fat, and their skin was as soft and supple as a teenager's. Knowing many arab countries had few restrictions against marrying much younger women, I wondered if they were even of legal age. As if that actually mattered out here in the middle of the desert.

Amir softened the strumming of his guitar and the girls eventually slowed their movement to a stop, then he turned toward me and smiled.

"What do you think of our traditional arab music and dance?" he said to me.

"It's beautiful," I said, shifting my position on the warm carpet, suddenly realizing how wet I'd become watching the two girls. "And very sensuous."

"Yes, it is," he said. "Do you have a particular request?"

I shook my head, unsure what he meant at first, then I cleared my throat when I realized he was talking about the music and not what I wanted to do with the girls.

"You mean like a Western *song*?"

"Yes," he nodded. "I always like to satisfy my guests' preferences."

I thought for a moment about a song that resonated with me that was also slow enough to fit with the girls' style of performance.

"Do you know the Bob Marley song Waiting in Vain, but played in the style of Annie Lennox?"

"Of course," he said. "It's one of my favorites."

He began strumming his guitar again, and the familiar melody of the song filled the tent while the two girls swayed their hips in harmony with the rhythm, clapping their castanets softly to provide gentle background accompaniment. A few moments later, Laila began humming the tune and Amir turned toward her, encouraging her to join him.

From the very first time I laid my eyes on you, girl, she sang with an angelic voice. *My heart said follow through. But I know, now, that I'm way down on your line...*

I turned to face her, amazed that she knew the lyrics to the song and enthralled by her gorgeous tone.

But the waiting feeling's fine, she cooed, meeting my gaze. *So don't treat me like a puppet on a string. 'Cause I know how to do my thing...*

Suddenly my thoughts echoed back to earlier in the day when she slipped my robe over my naked body, and the way she peered at me as she leaned in toward me.

Had she felt the same sexual attraction I'd had for her when we first met?

As she sang the words, she looked into my eyes and smiled while I tapped my feet rhythmically against the soft carpet.

I don't want to wait in vain for your love, she sang, gazing at me directly as my mouth parted in a spellbinding stupor. Suddenly, I couldn't wait to get out of Amir's tent and back into the women's enclosure where I could lie next to her on the warm desert sand under my soft wool cape.

As the song wound down and the girls' movement slowed to a stop, Amir placed his guitar to one side and reached around behind him, placing two odd-looking drums on the mat in front of him. Made of different-sized hollowed-out ceramic bowls with dried animal skins stretched over top, they looked like homemade bongo drums. As if on cue, Laila reached beside her and picked up a wooden reed instrument fashioned in the manner of a flared flute.

"That was beautiful," I said, peering at the two of them. "I don't think I've enjoyed that song as much as I did just now. This whole experience has been a feast for the senses."

Amir smiled as he pulled the drums in closer toward his knees.

"I'd like to finish with song I wrote myself for this kind of occasion," he said. "Unfortunately, I can't sing as well as Laila and her mouth will be otherwise occupied during this tune, so you'll just have to enjoy the *other* elements of the performance," he said, nodding toward the two belly dancers.

As he began beating on the drums with two hands, Laila picked up the flute-shaped instrument and began humming another arabic tune, tapping her fingers rhythmically over the holes on top of the shaft. The girls began swinging their hips slowly at first, but as Amir began increasing the pace of his tapping, they gyrated their hips faster and faster, turning their bodies around as I watched their buttock muscles flexing and shaking under the silk tassels hanging down from their tight bikini bottoms. As Laila matched Amir's escalating backbeat in pace and volume, the girls grew increasingly animated with the shaking of their bodies, looking like they were building up to some kind of climax.

While they shook their bodies with increasing passion and fervor in the form of a simulated sex act, I found myself shifting my weight again on the warm carpet underneath me, growing progressively wetter from their suggestive body movements and facial expressions. Amir became increasingly energetic pounding his drums with his two hands, and I noticed that he was staring at the girls with a lustful look in his eyes. The sexual tension in the room was now at a fever pitch, and as he banged out the last part of the performance, I saw a light sweat dripping over his brow. When he finished the song with two loud bangs on the drums, for a few moments everything in the tent became still as I listened to the sound of everyone's heavy breathing.

"Did you enjoy our little performance this evening?" he said, turning to face me after a long pause.

"Yes, very much," I panted, suddenly realizing how much the performance had raised my *own* heartbeat.

"If you'll excuse me now," he said, looking at the two scantily clad girls in front of him and motioning for them to stay behind. "I think it's time for me to turn in now. Laila will look after your sleeping arrangements. I'll see you again in the morning."

"Thank you," I said, as Laila and I stood to leave. "I'm sure I'll sleep very soundly this evening."

When I followed Laila out the front flap of Amir's tent, I noticed a dark shadow moving away from the perimeter and I recognized Ali's shape in the flickering moonlight. I shook my head realizing that he'd been spying on the erotic performance through a hole in the tent and picked up my pace to catch up with Laila.

"It's as simple as *that*, is it?" I said, referring to Amir's unbridled control over the girls. "He only has to nod, and the women submit to whatever his request?"

"Unfortunately, yes," she said, peering at me with sad eyes. "He's bought and paid for us, and we have to do whatever he says."

"Even if that means sleeping with him whenever he demands?"

"*Especially* that," she said.

"You seem somewhat less eager than the other girls," I said.

"He's had his way plenty enough times with me," she shrugged. "Thankfully, he now prefers the younger girls. Did you at least enjoy the performance?"

"Yes," I said. "It was very–*stimulating*. But honestly, I enjoyed your singing more than anything else. You have a gorgeous voice. Even when you played the wind instrument, I couldn't take my eyes off of you."

"Thank you," she said, noticing me pull my wool shawl over my shoulders to protect against the biting desert wind. "You have a very intoxicating manner about you as well. Come, let's get out of this cold desert air and bundled underneath something warmer."

When we entered the women's tent, all the other girls were already lying fast asleep on their blankets on the sand, with only one small open spot left in the corner of the enclosure. Laila laid a large blanket down over the space, then nonchalantly pulled her dress up over her shoulders, folding the robe and headdress on the ground next to the blanket. I couldn't help staring at her voluptuous body, highlighted by the lone flickering candle next to the makeshift bed. Her breasts were full and firm, resting high on her chest with dark medallions encircling her thick, pointed nipples. Her bare hips curved sensuously around the dark patch of pubic hair on her mound, tapering to long but muscular legs. In the dark shadows of the enclosed pavilion, she looked to me like some kind of sexy Amazon.

Then she picked up a large woolen blanket and threw it over her shoulders, lying down on the carpet peering up at me.

"Are you just going to stand there, or are you going to get under the covers and help keep me warm?"

"In the *buff*?" I said, unsure what the proper protocol was for women sleeping together in the tight confines of the communal tent.

"It's more comfortable that way," she said. "The less washing of our clothes that we have to do, the better. We prefer to air them out overnight. Besides, the sheepskin feels so much better against your bare skin. Come join me if you feel brave enough."

I pulled off my shawl and lifted my thawb over my shoulders, placing them gently on the sand on the other side of the blanket, then lifted the fluffy duvet and nestled in next to her.

"Oh, I'm feeling brave enough," I said, turning to face her.

"Good," she said. "Because those dancing girls weren't the *only* thing distracting my attention this evening."

5

───────

Laila turned her body toward me, then shifted her weight closer, wrapping her legs around my hips. I could feel her soft bush caressing my bare mound as she pressed her breasts firmly against my chest. I placed my hand against the side of her head and leaned in to kiss her, and our tongues melded together in a different kind of erotic dance.

"Laila," I whispered. "I'm so happy we have a chance to sleep together. I've wanted you from the moment I laid eyes on you."

"Why do you think I joined the two of you in Amir's tent?" she said, smiling into my eyes. "I wanted you all to myself."

"Weren't you worried that I might have stayed with *him* instead?"

"Possibly," she cooed. "He certainly knows how to put on the charm when he wants something."

"I already made it clear to him that I didn't come here for *romantic* reasons," I said. "Besides, men don't really do it for me any longer."

"Oh?" she said. "You prefer the company of women?"

"Only *certain* ones," I purred, grinding my pussy against hers.

"Do you mind if I examine you more closely?" she said. "I've never seen a Western woman up close and naked before. You're very–*different*."

"Absolutely," I said. "I've been fantasizing about you strumming your fingers over something other than that *flute* for the last half hour."

"Mmm," she groaned, moving further under the blanket.

As she nibbled her way down my body, I felt her hard nipples etching a line over my trembling stomach. When her mouth reached my breasts, she circled my teats with her warm tongue then sucked them hard into her mouth as she squeezed my mounds with both hands. Unlike the tender manner of most new lovers, I reveled in her rough and dominant style of lovemaking. If this was the way arab women made love to one another, I was ready to be taken.

I placed my hands on the back of her head and pulled her harder against my chest, burying her face between my cleavage. Then I lifted my right knee and pressed it between her splayed legs until it stopped against her wet vulva. She sighed as I began to rock my hips forward and back, stretching the skin of my thigh over her burning pussy.

"Lick me down below," I panted, rolling my hips frantically against her belly. "I need to feel your hot lips on my pussy before I explode."

"Soon enough," she said, blowing softly on my belly as she inched her way down toward my aching snatch.

But when her face reached my shaved mound she paused, feeling my bare skin while she rolled the sides of her cheeks against my soft flesh, kissing me softly at the apex of my slit where my labia merged together at the top of my clit.

"Oh *God* yes," I panted, feeling her warm lips touching my sensitive organ for the first time. "Lick my slit and taste my juices. See how wet you've made me."

She pressed her head a few inches lower, then ran her flat tongue over the length of my folds, lapping up my dripping juices.

"Yes, I can see that," she purred. "You taste much better than goat's milk over rice."

"Yes," I gasped. "Suck on me like a tender lamb. I want to feel your tongue probing every part of me."

Laila curled her tongue as she mashed her face between my legs, pressing it deep into my hole. I grabbed her head, pulling her harder against my cunt, rubbing her face up and down my dripping crease. There was something about the raw act of fucking her naked on the desert sand that I found incredibly arousing. Seeing her wrapped up in her full body covering and suddenly feeling her naked body writhing next to mine took me to new heights of pleasure.

"Mmm," I groaned. "I need you to suck my button now. I want to feel your tongue on my clit. Suck me, Laila."

"Hmm," she purred, moving her head higher up on my slit.

When she surrounded my jewel with her lips I almost came right away, but she seemed to sense my heightened state of arousal and for a long moment she held her head still between my legs while she felt my clit pulsing in her mouth. But when she began rolling her tongue over my nub in slow sensuous arcs, bathing me with her warm saliva, I couldn't help moaning out loud.

"God, yes," I panted. "That feels so good. I needed this so badly."

"Mmm-hmm," Laila nodded, feeling my juices running down her chin and neck.

I could feel my passion beginning to rise and I could have come quite easily from the action of her tongue alone on my raging clit, but what she did next took me to an entirely new level of ecstasy. She slipped two fingers of her right hand into my hole and buried them knuckle deep while stretching her little finger further down my perineum and circling it over my tender anus.

Fuck me, I thought. *This girl really knows how to make love to a woman.* I wondered just how much extra-curricular activity went on at night in the privacy of the women's tent while the other men were sleeping. I had no idea, but I was certainly interested in finding out.

When she began curling the two fingers inside me toward my G-spot, I arched my back and began grunting like a wild animal. I couldn't hold back the floodgate of pleasure any longer as my orgasm suddenly overtook me like a freight train.

"Yes, Laila!" I wailed. "I'm going to come, baby. I'm going to come all over your pretty face."

Part of me wanted to warn Laila about my tendency to squirt when I was this wet and worked up, but there wasn't any time. I suddenly felt the muscles of my pussy begin to clench uncontrollably, gushing my pent-up juices all over her slippery face and the soft blanket below us.

"Uhnn," she groaned, seeming to enjoy my orgasm almost as much as I was while she felt the walls of my pussy contracting powerfully on her fingers still deeply embedded inside me.

It must have taken over a full minute for me to stop coming in her arms with the most powerful orgasm I'd had in months. When I finally began to calm down, I collapsed onto the moist blanket and turned to kiss her softly on her lips.

"Thank you," I said, running my fingers through her hair. "I really needed that."

"You seemed to be already pretty worked up. Did you get that excited watching the two girls performing their special dance?"

"I have to admit that I did," I nodded. "I don't know if it was because I was so surprised to see their almost naked figures or because of the way they were moving their bodies, but it didn't just put *Amir* in the mood for some extra nighttime fun."

"So you're attracted to women also?"

"Definitely," I said. "I find women are more adept at satisfying my sexual needs, just as you were a few moments ago. In fact, your special expertise suggests this wasn't the first time you've made love to a woman either."

"Of course not," she smiled. "What do you think we girls do with ourselves in this tent when we're left to our own devices?"

"*All* of you?" I asked, feeling my juices dripping out of my slit once again at the thought of the pretty girls having a group orgy in their little pleasure dome.

"Um-hm," Laila nodded. "There are twenty women but only one penis in our traveling caravan. How *else* do you think we satisfy our needs?"

"What about poor Ali?" I said. "Isn't he ever allowed to get in on the action?"

"Amir would never share the women he's bought and paid for with another man. It would be considered a violation punishable by death if he so much as *looked* at one of us the wrong way. Besides, with his hooked nose and foul-smelling breath, none of us would ever be interested in him that way."

"Well I'm certainly interested in *you* that way," I smiled, threading my thigh again between her legs toward her steaming pussy. "It's my turn to give you the kind of pleasure you just administered to me."

As I began to move my body lower under the blanket, Laila suddenly stopped me, flipping me over onto my back.

"Why don't we *both* share the pleasure this time?" she said, rolling her body on top of me and lifting my left leg while she pressed her wet vulva against my pussy.

"If you insist," I said, smiling up at her.

"I want to watch you this time while I make love to you," she said. "I've never made love to a white girl before."

I smiled at her reference to me as a white girl, even though we were both technically caucasian. But there was no denying that she was considerably darker than me, and I felt a similar sexual attraction to her exotic appearance.

"I'm sure it's not so different from the *other* girls you've fucked," I said, feeling her thick bush pressing against my bald pubis. "Other than being *bare* down there."

"Like a little girl," she grunted, beginning to grind her twat against mine.

"Does that turn you on?" I said, reaching up to pinch her thick nipples as her large breasts swayed overtop my chest.

"Maybe," she said. "I've never felt a woman's bare *kus* before."

"Not even when you experimented when you were younger?"

"Never like *this*," she panted, rocking her hips more rapidly against mine as the sound of our wet pussies slapping together filled the cabin.

"Fuck my girly pussy, Laila," I teased her, recognizing that she was getting turned on by the naughty imagery. "I want to gush all over your furry snatch when we come this time."

"Yes," she huffed, throwing her head back in pleasure as we squeezed each other's breasts tightly with both hands. "You're so wet and slippery down there. I like the feeling of your bare sex against me."

"Would you like to try it yourself sometime?" I said, lifting my hand to her face as she sucked my thumb into her mouth. "Perhaps I can groom you myself while I'm here."

"I'm not sure Amir would appreciate me defiling my body in a way that's not in accordance with muslim custom."

"But you already said he rarely shows interest in you that way. This can just be between the two of us. It will grow back within a few weeks after I leave."

"I'm not sure I'm going to *want* you to leave after this," she said, pulling my leg up higher as she wrapped her arms around it, pulling it tightly between her sweating breasts. "Come with me, Jade. I want to feel your juices mingling with mine when you climax this time."

"*Fuck* yes," I panted, just waiting for her signal. "Grind your pussy against mine. I'm going to cum all over your hairy bush. Here it comes, baby."

"Uhnnn!" Laila suddenly grunted, throwing her head back in rapture, and for the second time that evening, I felt my body pushing over the precipice as another powerful orgasm washed over me and I began squirting jets of liquid all over Laila's twitching pussy.

As we watched each other's bodies convulsing atop one another in the dim light of the tent, I suddenly heard the soft squealing sounds of the other women around us while they pleasured themselves listening to the two of us. Something told me my little caravan excursion was about to stretch out into a longer adventure than I'd planned.

6

———————

The following morning, Laila and I rose at the break of dawn and got dressed, heading outside for breakfast. Amir was already sitting around the fire pit with a scattering of women preparing the meal. He smiled when he recognized me wearing my thawb and invited the two of us to sit beside him.

"Did you sleep well last night?" he asked me.

"Yes, thank you," I said. "I found it surprisingly comfortable sleeping on the desert sand."

"It's fine as long as you have a thick blanket underneath you. The grains have a way of finding their way into every nook and cranny of your body if you're not careful out here. I prefer to sleep a few inches off the surface myself."

I peered around the circle and recognized the two girls from last night's belly dance performance back in their long robes and headdresses, baking flatbread atop a curved metal hotplate.

"That smells wonderful, whatever it is you're making," I said, choosing to ignore his none-too-subtle intimation about our sleeping arrangements.

"Fresh flatbread and yogurt," he said, motioning to the tall trees surrounding the encampment. "With a side portion of dates, harvested directly from these palm trees."

I shook my head in awe at the simplicity of their nomadic lifestyle.

"I'm amazed how self-sufficient you can be simply from what you carry with you across the desert."

"Yes," he nodded. "Our goats provide milk, cheese, and yogurt, and the sheep provide all the meat we need. Everything else is supplied by the markets we visit along the fringe of the desert on our caravan route."

"If you don't mind my asking," I said, watching the women flipping the sizzling flatbread over the metal hotplate. "How do you pay for the extra materials? I mean, how do you earn hard *currency* while traveling across the desert?"

"Primarily from our livestock," Amir said. "Our animals are quite prolific, and there's a strong demand for these animals wherever we go. The camels in particular are very valuable commodities since they live for so long and can travel long distances without any water."

I glanced at the herd of camels grazing on the sparse grass and drinking from a wooden trough next to the well.

"And they're able to carry your entire entourage with all of its regalia across the open desert?"

"Yes, they're very strong and hardy animals. We'd never be able to survive out here in the middle of the desert without them."

The girls placed some of the fresh flatbread on individual plates along with bowls of yoghurt and chopped dates, then passed them around the circle to the now fully assembled group.

"Please—eat up," Amir said. "You'll need your strength if you plan to stay with us a little longer. The desert provides, but it also takes away. Your body burns a lot more calories in this sweltering heat."

I watched him dip his flatbread into the bowl of yogurt and pick up the dates with his fingers, and I followed his lead. Everything tasted incredibly fresh and delicious and when I finished my plate, I licked my fingers clean like the rest of the group.

"Oh my God," I sighed. "I could get used to this way of life. Everything is so simple and easy out here. Even the food tastes better than what I'm used to at many five-star restaurants. Talk about farm to table!"

"Are you enjoying it enough to *join* us on the next leg of trip to Algiers?" Amir smiled.

I paused for a moment, remembering what I'd told Hannah before I left my hotel in Marrakesh.

"How far away is it? I told my friends they should expect to hear back from me in a few days."

"It six or seven days by camel ride. But we'll be sleeping out in the open most nights under the stars. We only set up camp when we stop near towns or at the few oases along our route."

"I think I can manage that," I nodded, smiling at Laila remembering how much I enjoyed sleeping next to her on the warm sand last night. "But only if you let me help clean and pack up like everyone else. If I'm going to join your troupe for a few days, I want to feel like a productive member of the tribe."

"If that's what you wish," Amir nodded. "Laila and Ali can look after whatever you need. Will you have any trouble making return travel arrangements from Algiers?"

"It shouldn't be a problem," I said. "As long as it has an international airport."

"Indeed it does," he said, standing to leave. "I'm going to collect my things while Ali begins dismantling the tents. We'll be setting out within the next hour."

I was surprised how quickly the group broke down the camp, neatly arranging all the tent poles, coverings, and contents atop the backs of the camels. When we were ready to leave, we filled our saddlebags with enough water to last us for a few days, then we headed east two-abreast atop the remaining camels. It was quite a sight watching the long train of animals traipsing through the pretty sand ripples lining the undulating desert with nothing to keep us occupied but the shifting shadows of the sun and the howling desert wind.

At nighttime, we circled the camels and livestock around us to provide a modicum of cover from the blowing breeze, then laid down on our individual blankets and woolen duvets to keep ourselves warm. I missed sleeping with Laila and more than once thought about sneaking under the covers to join her, but I dared not risk disturbing Amir and Ali who were sleeping nearby.

After three days, we came upon another small oasis and set up the tents once again to provide a respite against the searing overhead sun. I was thrilled to have another chance to make love to Laila in the relative privacy of our own tent, and after the girls fell asleep, she let me shave her mound with the travel razor I'd packed in my bag, using goat's milk and yogurt as an improvised shaving cream. Afterwards, I licked her clean as she knelt over my face writhing in pleasure while I sucked her bare vulva and clit into my mouth.

But the following morning, something happened that forever changed the course of my dreamlike desert adventure. As I flipped open the flap of our tent to fetch some water from the well, I noticed Fatima, one of the girls who'd performed the belly dance a few nights earlier, lifting a pail out of the well while Ali snuck up behind her, trying to lift her robe while he pulled his erect penis out from under his kaftan. When she ducked aside to evade his unwanted advance, he suddenly lost his balance and tumbled head over heels into the well, screaming all the way down until I heard a loud splash when he fell unconscious at the bottom of the pit. Fatima looked around her with frightened eyes and we she saw me watching, she rushed toward me crying, throwing her arms around me wailing in arabic.

Not wanting her to be discovered, I ushered her quickly into our tent and explained to Laila what had happened. A few seconds later, Amir emerged from his tent alarmed by the commotion, calling out Ali's name. Suspicious when he didn't immediately hear his reply, Amir went back into his tent and came out carrying a flashlight, pointing it down into the well. When he saw Ali's body floating face-down in the pool of water, he turned toward our tent and stormed toward it, angrily flipping open the door covering.

He glared at Laila with steely eyes and a red face, speaking loudly to her in arabic. She said something back to him and shrugged her shoulders, feigning ignorance at what had just transpired. He then approached each of the girls separately, asking them if they knew what had happened. But we got to Fatima, he noticed that she was shaking and he placed his hand under her chin, raising her face to meet his angry gaze. She shook her head, afraid to admit any involvement in the incident, but when he saw her dried tear tracks, he grabbed her hair, dragging her outside.

I looked at Laila bewildered and asked what was going on.

"It's not good," she said, following Amir outside. "Just stay close to me and don't say anything."

"Why don't we just tell him the *truth*?" I said. "That it was an innocent mistake, and that she was just trying to protect herself from Ali's unwanted advance?"

"It doesn't work that way," Laila said, shaking her head. "The scales of justice are tipped greatly in favor of the men in our culture. If she were discovered to have been involved in his death, even incidentally, it wouldn't end well for her."

"So what happens if nobody's willing to talk?"

Laila gritted her teeth as she watched Amir remove his long curved knife from under his belt and place it over the fire. I watched the steel grow red-hot in the flame, then he pulled Fatima's head back and placed the hot blade next to her face. He said something angrily to her and she shook her head frighteningly. Then he forced her mouth open as she slowly extended her tongue. He placed the flat side of the knife on it and she screamed as the blade made a horrible sizzling sound against her flesh.

"What the *fuck*..." I said, stepping toward her trying to intercede.

"Don't," Laila said, grabbing my arm.

"But what he's doing to her in *inhuman*," I protested. "She's just an innocent bystander–"

"This is the way justice is administered in the bedouin culture. When there's a dispute involving a serious crime and no one comes forward to admit guilt, the men administer what is called a *bisha'a*, which is a type of trial by ordeal. The accused person is forced to lick a hot piece of metal and if the tongue shows any sign of a burn or a scar, this is considered a sign of guilt."

"Of *course* her tongue will burn!" I exclaimed. "He just placed a red-hot *knife* against her flesh!"

Amir removed the knife from Fatima's mouth, then doused her tongue with a ladle of fresh water. Then he peered closely at it and threw her down on the sand, cursing at her in their native tongue.

"So what happens now?" I said to Laila.

"If a woman is convicted of this type of crime, she's usually sentenced to death, often by public stoning. But Amir won't do it himself. He'll have to take her to a local tribal court where judgement will be formally handed down and administered by the muslim council."

"You've got to be kidding me," I said, hardly believing what I'd just seen and heard.

Amir turned around noticing that Laila and I had witnessed the entire scene, and walked toward us with flaring nostrils.

"I'm sorry you had to see that," he said to me. "But what Fatima did was a serious crime that cannot be ignored. She will have to face the consequences of her actions. Laila, I want you to coordinate with the other women so we can pack up the camp immediately. We'll be heading out to Algiers as soon as possible to have Fatima's fate decided."

"Wait!" I said, stepping toward Amir in desperation. "I saw the whole thing. She didn't do anything wrong. Ali assaulted her and she was simply trying to defend herself. It was just an accident when he tripped and fell into the well."

Amir paused for a moment as his eyes flashed over my beseeching face, then he shook his head dismissively.

"She must have done something to provoke him," he said. "He couldn't have fallen so easily into the well. We will see what the tribal council decides in Algiers."

"And if she's found guilty?" I said.

"She'll be put to death immediately," Amir said, turning to head back to his tent.

I tried to follow after him, but Laila grabbed my robe, holding me back.

"He can't get away with that!" I said, turning toward her. "It's barbaric!"

"Unfortunately, this is the way of our culture. If a muslim woman is even *suspected* of fraternizing inappropriately with a man other than her husband, Sharia law dictates that she be summarily executed."

"By public *stoning*? What about the guilt of the *man*? What if it's simply one person's word over another?"

"In our culture, the man is always presumed innocent since they have free rein over the women and females are instructed to refrain from fraternizing with anyone other than their husbands."

"I'd hardly refer to what they were doing at the well as *fraternizing*. There's only one place for everybody to collect water out here. It's inevitable that there'll be some form of close contact among such a small group in close quarters. Surely something can be done–"

"I'm afraid we have no control over the situation," Laila said, looking at me sadly. "It's out of our hands now."

Later that evening, we stopped in the middle of the desert to rest for the night and grab a bite to eat, and everybody sat around the campfire looking sadly at each other. Nobody dared say a thing, knowing full well what Amir's intentions were. I peered at Fatima, shivering next to the fire as Laila wrapped her arms around her, trying to provide a modicum of comfort. When we dispersed after the meal to make our individual beds in the sand, I took Laila aside and peered into her eyes.

"We can't just let this poor girl be unjustly punished for a crime she didn't commit," I pleaded.

"What would you have us do?" she said. "*He's* the one with all the power and the control. We can't just overpower him and run away."

I crossed my arms and shook my head at the absurdity of the situation.

Laila paused for a long moment, then looked up at me through narrowed eyelids.

"There might be *another* way we can extricate ourselves from this unfortunate situation," she said. "What if we steal away in the middle of the night and take all the camels with us? He won't be able to follow us, and he'll run out of water long before he gets to Algiers."

"But he'd *die* out here in the middle of the desert without any food or water!" I said.

"It's either him or Fatima," she said. "Who do you think is more deserving to live? The innocent girl who did nothing other than try to protect herself from a violent rape, or the man who summarily judges her based on his ludicrous code of honor?"

"But he seemed to be so–"

"Sophisticated, and a man of the world?" Laila said. "There are two sides to every man, and this one is no different. He may have been educated in your country, but I assure you that his morals and underlying character have been indelibly shaped by his family affiliations and the culture of his tribe. Are you prepared to do what has to be done?"

I paused for a moment, trying to think of any other conceivable options, then I grudgingly nodded. I couldn't believe that my exciting desert adventure had suddenly turned into a deadly serious conspiracy where two people's lives lay in the balance.

7

————

Laila and I waited until we heard Amir snoring under his blanket, then she roused each of the girls, telling them about our escape plan. Everybody got up and tiptoed through the sand toward the camels, then we tethered them together and mounted them carefully, slowly leading them away from the rest of the livestock herd.

"What about the goats and the sheep?" I whispered into Laila's ear, who I'd paired up with on the lead camel.

"We haven't got time to gather them together and we can't risk disturbing Amir–"

Suddenly I heard a man's voice yelling in the darkness, and I turned to see Amir rising from his sleep and begin chasing after us. Laila kicked the sides of her camel and the whole train burst into a gallop, creating a dusty trail behind us. Amir screamed and shook his fists as he tried to catch up with us, but he was no match for the fleet group of camels, and within seconds he disappeared behind us in the thick cloud of dust.

"*Jesus,*" I said to Laila after we'd put a few hundred meters between us. "Are you sure this is going to work? Now we're *all* unwitting accomplices in this sordid affair."

"We're at least three days' camel ride to the nearest village on the outskirts of the desert," she said. "It would take three times as long to cover that distance on foot. There's no way he can survive in this stifling heat for that long without water."

"And the *rest* of the animals?"

"They're a bit more hardy. We can come back for them a little later when the coast is clear."

I peered behind me to see the other girls following behind Laila's camel in single file.

"What will you and the others do now that you're no longer part of Amir's caravan?"

"I plan to send them back home to their families when we get to Algiers. This many camels will fetch more than enough money to arrange safe transit to their home ports."

"What about *you*? Won't people be looking for Amir at some point if he doesn't show up? Surely his family–"

"I plan to be long gone before anyone raises any suspicions. I've got some extended family in the Andalusia region of Spain where I can lay low for a while. I'm more worried about you. Did you tell anyone that you were going to join Amir's caravan? The local authorities won't take kindly to finding out you might have been involved somehow in his disappearance."

I paused for a moment trying to remember the details of the message I'd sent Hannah before I set off to see Amir at the cafe.

"Just my best friend back home," I said. "I gave her Amir's name and told her to alert the U.S. Embassy in Morocco if she didn't hear from me in a week or so."

"You'd best clear out of this region at your earliest opportunity then," she said. "It will be difficult for the local police to hold you to account once you're out of the country."

"But I didn't do anything–" I began to protest.

"We're *all* implicated now. If they find Amir's dead body, they could trace any one of us to the deed. Technically, we'd all be considered accessories to the crime."

"Christ," I sighed, feeling my heart suddenly racing at the implications of what we'd done. "What the hell have I gotten myself into?"

"Don't worry," Laila said, patting my thigh reassuringly. "The desert soon buries anything that doesn't move. He'll never be found, and we'll all be long gone before anyone raises any suspicions."

"What about *Ali*?" I said. "Won't another caravan eventually find his dead body at the bottom of the well?"

"Perhaps, but with any luck it should be pretty decomposed by then. Whoever finds him will have difficulty connecting him to Amir's disappearance."

Suddenly I had a queasy feeling in the pit of my stomach, and I wrapped my arms around Laila's midsection, resting my head against her back as I peered at the never-ending hills of red sand dunes.

"How will you find your way through this wasteland all the way to Algiers?" I asked.

"The shadows of our camels will guide the way. It shows which way the sun is pointed, and all we have to do is head east and north until we reach the Mediterranean coast. From there, it should be easy to track our way to the city."

"You're a pretty smart cookie," I smiled, clutching her closely. "These girls were pretty lucky to have such a strong leader to get them out of this predicament."

"I hope they'll be happier now that they're freed from Amir's grip," she nodded. "But I'll be sad to see some of them go. I've grown quite attached to these girls after all this time we've spent together in the desert."

Twelve hours later, the sun began to fade over the horizon and Laila stopped the group to set up camp, laying out our bedrolls amongst the circle of resting camels. Most of our food was still packed in the saddlebags and we enjoyed a peaceful dinner of rice, cooked legumes, and sweet dates. Everybody seemed much more relaxed around the campfire, chatting and giggling amongst themselves in their native arabic.

When we finished eating, we retired to our beds but soon discovered in our haste to leave the previous camp that we hadn't brought enough bedrolls and blankets for everybody to sleep on separately. Taking charge of the situation as always, Laila nestled the blankets together then we lay down as a group, not bothering to take off our robes to protect ourselves against the encroaching desert chill. It didn't take long for everyone to snuggle together for extra warmth, and before long I felt the telltale sensation of someone's fingers sliding up the bottom of my smock.

I turned around and saw Fatima smiling at me in the soft moonlight, and she leaned in to kiss me. Whether she was trying to express her gratitude for my helping to save her or she was just curious about feeling my fair skin, I couldn't be sure. But either way, I was happy to accommodate her newfound intimate interest in me. As we began to kiss more passionately, intertwining our tongues and pressing our bodies together, she pulled my robe up over my hips, caressing the outside of my thighs and my round buttocks.

But when her hand curved around to my bald pubis, she gasped and uttered something in arabic. I heard Laila reply to her in the darkness on my other side, and Fatima giggled as Laila rolled over to sandwich me between the two of them. Suddenly I had two pairs of hands caressing my body from both sides, and I moaned as they slipped their fingers between my thighs, caressing my vulva from two ends. I pulled Fatima's smock higher, feeling her fluffy bush caressing my bare mound, and I groaned in her mouth as her fingers found my pleasure spot and she began rubbing my clit in soft circular motions. But when I felt Laila's fingers press inside my slit and begin fingerfucking me from behind, I began rocking my hips, moaning more loudly.

When the rest of the girls began to realize what the three of us were up to, it didn't take long for the entire group to devolve into a moaning, slithering mass of naked bodies writhing under the thick jumble of cotton robes and woolen blankets. I pulled Fatima's dress all the way over her shoulders and squeezed her bare tits while she played with my clit and moaned into my mouth. It didn't take long for the combined action of her manipulation of my clit and Laila's caressing of my vulva to bring me to the brink of pleasure. As the two women pressed their bodies tightly against mine, I felt my orgasm overtake me and I jerked my body spastically, gushing all over the two girl's hands.

Fatima said something again to Laila, and she responded in arabic, then Fatima moved her body down closer to my midsection, apparently fascinated by my unusual bare mound and my propensity to squirt when I came. When she spread my legs apart, the other girls stopped what they were doing to peer at my dripping bald pussy glistening in the moonlight. Before I knew it, I had a clutch of pretty young girls kissing and probing every part of my body as Laila propped her head up on her elbow, smiling at me.

"Holy shit," I said to her. "You weren't kidding about how these girls like to stay entertained when the men aren't around. I think I've died and gone to *heaven!*"

"Welcome to the club, baby," Laila said, leaning in to kiss me as I felt a deluge of tongues and fingers converging on me while they sucked and nibbled on every square inch of my body. The multitude of erotic sensations soon brought me to the edge again, and I screamed in ecstasy as my whole body convulsed in another intense orgasm. Fatima suddenly pulled away from licking me while the whole group watched my pussy twitching and squirting my juices all over her face and my bare legs.

"Oh my God," I purred to Laila, after I came down from my high. "I could seriously get used to this. Are you *sure* you want to disband this group of horny young vixens?"

"Not for a couple more *days* at least," she smiled, rolling her body on top of me, grinding her dripping mound into my pliant face.

As I began to eat her pussy, the girls swarmed over top of me like a bunch of buzzing bees, rubbing their wet pussies and hairy bushes over whatever open flesh they could find on my pinned body. One of them positioned herself between my legs, pulling her pussy tight against mine and began scissoring me in a prone 'X' position while some of the other girls sucked my nipples and toes. Before we all fell asleep in a steaming pile of sweaty flesh, I must have come at least a dozen more times sucking, caressing, and fucking every one of the girls in one position or another.

As I lay on the soft desert sand surrounded by the bevy of beautiful women, I looked up toward the sky at the cloud of stars shimmering above me like a blanket of sparkling sequins. Suddenly the troubles at the previous camp seemed a hundred miles away, and I smiled at one of Amir's last comments to me. *The desert gives and takes away indeed*, I thought, as I drifted off to sleep.

8

For the next couple of days, we rode slowly through the desert, stopping periodically to relieve ourselves and snack on dried dates and flatbread. At night we reassembled the blankets in one large group and resumed our wild orgy under the stars until we all fell asleep, completely spent and satiated. I almost regretted seeing the dusty buildings on the edge of Algiers as we approached the city from the west, and I squeezed Laila's tummy softly to express how much I dreaded the thought of leaving her.

She parked me and the rest of the girls out of sight behind a tall dune so as not to arouse suspicion, then she led the camels three at a time into the local trading market, where she sold them at a relative bargain. It was approaching dusk by the time she returned to fetch all of us, then she took us down to the docks to arrange clandestine travel for each of the girls to return to their original towns. She gave each of them enough money to pay for the remainder of their passage, then the two of us walked along the waterfront while we talked about our next steps.

"That looked easier than I *thought* it would be," I said after all of the girls had boarded their individual ships to head home.

"These merchant seamen will transport anything for the right amount of money," she nodded.

"What about the harbormaster? How did you manage to bypass all the usual paperwork and document controls?"

"The protocols for onboarding and offboarding passengers on cargo ships are far looser on the North African coast than in Europe or America," she said, sliding her fingers and her thumb together to indicate the payment of a bribe. "Nobody seems to have a problem looking the other way as long as you grease their palms a little bit."

"How can you be sure the ships' captains will *complete* the transaction now that they've already been paid?"

"Because I promised to have them paid an *equivalent* amount once the girls safely complete their journey on the other end."

"All of this is made possible from the selling of a few *camels*?"

"Um-hm," Laila nodded. "Amir paid to take us *away* from our homes, now he's indirectly arranged to pay for them to get back."

"I'm not sure this was exactly the way he envisioned it," I frowned, trying not to think about how much he was suffering in the middle of the desert without any food or water.

"I suppose not," she chuckled. "Though I don't think *any* of this went down the way he imagined."

"So what now?" I said, peering over the Mediterranean as the sun began to set on the horizon.

"We pretend like none of this ever happened," she said. "You go back home to America, and I slip across the sea to start a new life in Spain. It shouldn't take long for us to put all of this unpleasantness behind us."

"It hasn't *all* been unpleasant," I said, grabbing her hand and pulling her into an alley to give her a long, passionate kiss. "I'll have far more *happy* memories to hold onto than this one unfortunate affair."

"Mmm," she nodded, pressing her body up tightly against me.

"Well isn't *this* a happy little reunion," a familiar man's voice suddenly cackled from the shadows.

Laila and I swung around to see Amir blocking the exit to the alley, brandishing his glinty curved knife.

"I knew the two of you were up to no good the moment I saw you ogling each other during the belly dance performance in my tent. And now it's time for the lot of you to be held to account for your transgressions. Right after you tell me what you've done with the other girls."

I stared at Amir with my mouth agape in a mix of shock and confusion.

"How–"

"Did I manage to get all this way on foot?" he said. "Your first mistake was leaving me with all the livestock. Their milk and meat can sustain a man for a long time in the desert. Plus, I was lucky enough to catch another passing caravan after a couple of days. If you two hadn't dawdled taking your time crossing the desert, you might have made a clean getaway by now." He paused, running his eyes up and down our bodies. "Of course, I didn't have any *other* distractions encouraging me to pause for a little entertainment in the evenings."

"So I suppose you've alerted the elders by now and arranged for us to be taken before the council to be properly punished?" Laila said, stepping in front of me and placing her arm around me protectively.

"In due course," he said. "First I needed to *find* you before you slipped away. I'm afraid your fate, along with the rest of my little harem, has already been sealed, Laila." Then he turned toward me, clucking his tongue. "As for my pretty Western friend, I'm sure we can find a dark prison somewhere in the bowels of this medieval city to let her rot away the rest of her miserable life."

Amir lurched forward, placing the knife under Laila's neck.

"Now *tell* me where the rest of the girls are!" he sneered.

Suddenly, Laila reared back, kicking Amir as hard as she could between his legs and he hunched over, dropping the knife onto the ground. She quickly picked it up and before he could regain his composure, she sliced it across the front of his neck in one quick and silent motion. He clutched his throat, looking at us with wild eyes, then he fell to his knees, collapsing onto the cobblestone pavement.

As a thick pool of blood seeped out of his jugular vein onto the darkened stones, the life slowly drained out of his eyes, and he suddenly became still.

"Holy *fuck*, Laila," I gasped. "You *killed* him!"

"It was either him or us," she said nonchalantly. "He got what was coming to him."

"What the hell do we do now?" I said, looking around frantically to see if anyone else had witnessed the scene. "We can't just *leave* him here. He can be traced back to us."

Laila paused for a moment as she peered around the wharf to get her bearings, then she nodded toward a nearby dock.

"We'll have to drag him to the edge of the jetty and dump him into the water. There's no one around and it's dark enough for us to dispose of the body. Grab a leg and help me pull him toward the pier."

I shook my head, hardly believing how fast our plan had unraveled and wondering what would happen if anyone saw us. But I knew Laila was right. Between the front desk attendant at my hotel in Morocco and my email trail to Hannah, there was more than enough circumstantial evidence to connect me to Amir's disappearance. The best chance for both of us to get away before the police caught wind of any malfeasance was to dispose of the body and exit as quickly as possible.

We each grabbed one of Amir's legs and after checking to make sure the coast was clear, we carefully dragged his body the thirty feet or so across the narrow roadway lining the wharf and dropped his lifeless body into the murky water at the edge of the pier. We watched his body slowly sink into the deep water, then we ducked into another alley to decide what to do next.

"So what do we do now?" I said, shivering from a combination of shock and the encroaching chill.

"You've still got your travel bag and papers," she said, nodding toward my clutch case. "You need to get changed back into your Western clothes as soon as possible and catch the earliest flight out of the country. With any luck, you'll be long gone before anyone finds any evidence of foul play. I'll pay for safe passage to the continent and try to slip into Spain undetected. Right now, we both have to get the hell out of here."

"Okay," I said, wrapping my arms around my body to keep myself from shaking. "But will I ever see you again? I hate leaving you this way..."

"It's best we make a clean break," she said, pulling me close against her breast. "We don't want anyone connecting us together after this. You'll be fine. I'll think of you whenever I'm sleeping alone under my woolen blanket."

I paused for a moment, darting my eyes across her pretty face. I hated the idea of leaving so abruptly, but I knew we didn't have any other choice. I opened my travel bag and scribbled my address on a piece of paper.

"This is my address back home in America," I said, handing her the paper. "Just do me one favor. Write me once you get situated in Spain and send me your address. It'll be safe to see you again once this all settles down. I'd love to be able to stay in touch."

"Okay," Laila said, folding the paper and tucking it away into her robe. "But you need to go now. I want you to catch the earliest flight out in the morning. I'll contact you once I get settled."

She leaned in towards me, clasping the sides of my head with both hands.

"This has been the most amazing adventure of my life," she said. "I'll never forget these few days we've shared together, my beautiful sweet, American girl. Safe travels, my love. We'll talk again soon."

Then she turned and walked briskly down the wharf into the inky darkness without looking back. I watched her robes billowing in the cool evening breeze until she disappeared in the mist, then I changed out of my thawb in the darkness of the alley and put my Western clothes back on, hailing a cab to the airport. I was lucky enough to catch the seven a.m. flight to Paris with a connecting flight to Chicago later that day. As my jet lifted off the runway and turned north over the Mediterranean Sea, I peered down at the wide expanse of sparking blue waves, smiling at how it reminded me of the golden sand ripples in the desert.

∿

After I got home, a few months passed without hearing from Laila, and I began to fear that she might not have made it out of the North Africa. But when I received an airmail letter postmarked Seville, Spain, I tore it open and read the contents breathlessly.

Jade,

I hope this letter finds you well and fully recovered from our little desert adventure. I've thought of you often since we departed so suddenly in Algiers and miss having your smooth, supple body snuggling up next to me. You may be happy to know that I've grown quite accustomed to your Western-style grooming habits and I always think of you whenever I touch myself on dark, lonely nights. If ever you find the time to come visit me, I've enclosed my new address below.

Love always, Laila

Oh my God, I exhaled, happy to hear that she'd made it out safely. And the fact that she still had fond memories of our time together and even thought of me whenever she touched herself intimately made my heart dance and my panties moisten. As I sat in my chair rereading her letter over and over again and smelling the delicate scent of jasmine and lemongrass infused in the paper, my fingers trailed a path down between my thighs as I separated my legs slowly.

Maybe this won't be the end of my arabian adventure after all, I smiled to myself.

THE SPA

AN EROTIC ADVENTURE

1

"What's up, girl?" my best friend Hannah said to me at our weekly lunch date. "You look a little run down. Have you been taking care of yourself?"

"I've been going to yoga class as often as I can, and I think I'm eating reasonably well. But I've kind of been flitting from one empty relationship to another, and I guess I'm in a bit of a rut."

"Mmm," Hannah nodded. "Maybe you need to break away from your routine for a change. You know, mix up the scenery, go somewhere you can relax and recharge your batteries."

"What did you have in mind?" I said.

"I've been thinking," she smiled with a slight curl of her lip. "I've heard about this new spa in town that takes a different slant on the whole wellness concept."

"How so?"

"Well, for one thing, it's for ladies only."

"That's nothing new. Ninety-five percent of the clientele at most spas is already women."

"This one's on the top floor of one of the tallest skyscrapers in Chicago. It's got a retractable roof and a beautiful open-air patio surrounding a huge pool with magnificent views of the city and the lake."

"That *does* sound a little more upscale than most," I nodded. "But if that's its big claim to fame, I'm not sure that's going to be enough to pull me out of my funk."

"What if I told you it's a *naked* spa?"

"What do you mean?" I said, suddenly intrigued. "You mean customers receive facials and massages in the nude?"

"Well yes, but it's much more than that. I mean *everybody's* naked, including in the common areas like the pool, sauna, and exercise studio."

"Really? Like a nudist camp or something?"

"A very *elite* nudist camp," she smiled. "With all the spa amenities. Where everybody is super wellness-oriented and in fabulous shape. Imagine sitting poolside watching all the hot women going in and out of the pool and cavorting in the hot tub."

I shifted unsteadily on my chair, suddenly realizing how wet my panties had become envisioning the scenario.

"Is there a *lot* of cavorting going on?"

"Let's just say it's a voyeur's paradise, where women are encouraged to mingle. From what I've heard, it's Chicago's answer to Plato's Retreat. There's allegedly a ton of extra-curricular activities going on. Don't tell me that doesn't get your juices going."

"Um–*yeah*," I said, feeling my pussy throb at the idea of an all-girls venue. "That does sound a little different. What about the staff? They don't have a problem with all that lewd socializing?"

"Quite the opposite. Apparently, they're just as involved in the delivery of the special services. Can you imagine getting a full-body massage with a hot masseuse with all the extra benefits? Or a Brazilian, or a pedicure, or a facial where they make sure you're satisfied in *every* possible way?"

I leaned back in my chair, scrunching up my face.

"Don't you think it would be kind of weird getting a wax where the aesthetician is focused on more than just cleaning things up down there?"

"You never know until you try," Hannah said. "Come on, Jade–you deserve to be pampered for a change. This is a place you can go where there's no judging, no expectations, no relationship pressures. You can indulge as little or as much as you wish in the carnal opportunities. Or just lie in the sun, go for a dip in the pool, and take in the scenery."

"The very *erotic* scenery," I smiled.

"That never stopped you before," she said, arching an eyebrow.

"Okay," I said. "You've twisted my arm. When did you have in mind for this little excursion?"

"Tomorrow at noon," she said, holding up two tickets. "I've already paid for both of us. My treat."

"Are you planning to be my wingwoman to keep me out of trouble?"

"Fuck *that*," Hannah chuckled. "I'm going to be your *partner-in-crime*, to make sure you get into as much trouble as possible."

2

———

The following day, I met Hannah in the lobby of an office tower on Magnificent Mile. It was a beautiful sunny day, and I could see all the way down Grand Avenue toward the Navy Pier and Lake Michigan. I was ready to forget my troubles and lose myself in the luxury and decadence of the upscale spa. I had no idea what I was in for, but the throbbing in my pussy suggested it would be anything but boring.

"So, are you ready for this?" Hannah said while we waited for the elevator on the ground floor.

"I think so," I said. "My *mind* isn't so sure, but my body seems to have other ideas."

We stepped into the lift and Hannah nodded, tapping the button for the sixty-third floor.

"I'm just as excited as you are to see what this is all about. My mind's been racing with all the possibilities ever since I bought the tickets."

"You had this planned for me all along, didn't you?" I said.

"Of course," Hannah smirked. "How could I not invite my bestie to the hottest show in town?"

When the elevator reached the top floor and the doors opened, I saw a pretty attendant dressed in a blue uniform sitting behind a frosted-glass desk flanked by a streaming water wall.

"It's impressive looking, that's for sure," I said. "But I thought you said all the staff were naked?"

"They have to present a professional face to the general public," Hannah said. "But I assure you, once we get behind the reception area, it will be an entirely different picture. Come on, let's check this place out."

We strolled up to the front counter, and the attendant looked up from her computer screen.

"Good afternoon," the girl said. "How can I be of service?"

"We have two day-passes," Hannah said, sliding the tickets over the counter.

"Of course," the girl said, peering at the tickets. "You're welcome to use all of our club's features at your leisure. There's the pool of course, the outdoor patio, the hot tub, sauna, and exercise studio. But if you wish to avail yourselves of the special services, you'll have to make an appointment."

"What services do you offer, specifically?"

"Our aestheticians and massage therapists provide facials, manicures/pedicures, massages, and intimate grooming."

Hannah turned toward me and smiled.

"What do you think, Jade? What would you like to do first?"

"I think I'm pretty good with the grooming. How about a massage?"

I looked toward the attendant.

"Do you offer doubles massages? When's your next opening?"

"We do," she said. "Our therapists are just finishing up with another appointment. They should be available in about twenty minutes if you'd both like to give it a try."

"Yes, thank you," Hannah nodded.

The attendant handed each of us a card key to enter the premises and separate locker keys.

"The change room is through the door to the left. Each of the service areas is clearly marked. The massage therapists will be waiting for you at one p.m."

"Is there a particular dress code while traveling about the common areas?" Hannah asked.

"You'll find a terrycloth robe in each of your lockers and two large bath towels. You're welcome to wear either of these in the common areas or nothing at all, if you prefer. We want you to feel as relaxed and comfortable as possible at all times. Most of our guests choose to relax in the nude, as they find that most liberating."

Liberating, indeed, I smiled at the attendant, noticing a gleam in her eye.

Hannah and I took our keys and passed through the locked guest door, then followed the signs to the change room. When we got there, there was a handful of women coming in and out of the showers, making little effort to conceal their naked bodies. Most of them looked to be in their twenties and early thirties, with well-toned figures and golden-brown skin.

"Looks like we're going be the old ladies of the bunch," Hannah chuckled, opening her locker next to mine.

"I'm okay with that," I said, taking off my clothes and hanging them in the locker next to the robe. "If this is any indication of what the rest of the customers look like, that'll work for me. Besides, we're no slouches. I think we can hold our own against the competition."

Hannah peered at a pretty blonde giving her the eye as she bent over to step out of her pants.

"Something tells me there's going to be a *lot* of holding our own against these ladies before the day is over," she winked.

I glanced at a slim African-American girl emerging from one of the showers. She had flawless caramel-colored skin and a model-perfect figure with firm, high breasts, a narrow waist, and an exquisitely rounded ass. As she patted her short afro dry, I stole a glance between her legs, watching the water drip down over her bald, brown mound.

"Jesus," I said. "I could jump any one of these girls right now. I hope these ladies are just getting *started* their spa treatment, not finishing."

"Not to worry," Hannah smiled, noticing me drooling at the pretty black girl. "I'm pretty sure there's lots more where those came from. Just try to keep your dick in your pants for a little longer while we ease our way into this experience."

"Whatever you say, boss," I said. "So what's the protocol? Do we wear our robes into the massage room or traipse around in the buff like everyone else it seems to be doing?"

"I don't see any harm in wearing the robe to start," Hannah said. "Besides, we need *somewhere* we store our locker keys."

"Come on," she said, glancing at her phone screen before placing it on the locker shelf and locking the door. "It's time for our massage."

I followed Hannah down the hall to the waiting area for the massages, where we sat in the plush chairs, picking up two copies of Vogue magazine lying on the adjacent tables. As I began leafing through the glamour shots of the gorgeous models, I wondered how many of them had frequented this place. The African-American girl I saw in the change room certainly could have qualified for any of these shoots, and I felt my nipples hardening at the idea of engaging with her later. After a few minutes, the door to the massage room opened and a nude brunette girl approached us.

She had a more athletic figure than the black girl from the locker room, but was equally stunning. With large, round tits and a perfectly toned stomach and bare midriff, my pussy began watering just looking at her.

"Are you Hannah and Jade for the one o'clock massage appointment?"

"Um, yes," I stammered, momentarily taken aback by her casual attitude and Amazonesque figure.

"Please," she said. "Come in."

When we entered the room, I saw a second attendant leaning over a sink washing her hands as her tight ass flexed over rippling hamstrings and calves. I looked at Hannah with wide eyes, mouthing the words *Holy Shit!* She peered back at me with an equally incredulous look, shrugging her shoulders.

"Just go with the flow, baby," she whispered.

In the middle of the room rested two side-by-side massage tables about four feet apart, covered with a long bath sheet and a rolled-up towel resting in the middle section.

"Can we hang your robes for you?" the brunette said as the blonde attendant turned around, drying her hands.

She was even more beautiful than the brunette, with long silky hair tied up in a bun and a slender figure with the most exquisite tits I'd seen in a long time. With her compact round ass, long slender legs, and mouth-wateringly curvy hips, she had the figure of a twenty-year-old stripper. I could feel the moisture rapidly building up between my legs as a trickle of lubrication dripped down the inside of my thigh.

"By all means," Hannah said, practically throwing her robe at the attendant.

"Make yourselves comfortable on the massage tables, facing face-down," the brunette said, obviously the more experienced of the two girls.

When I lay down on one of the benches, I was happy when I saw the blonde girl approach my table with a bottle of massage oil. I would have been happy to have either girl touch me, but there was something about the blonde one that got my juices flowing. As I watched the brunette hovering over Hannah's naked body pouring oil into her hands, I glanced at Hannah with wide eyes. Neither of us had to say a word, since both of us were thinking the same thing. This was as close to heaven as two living and breathing people surely could have gotten.

When I felt the blonde's slippery hands run up my spine starting from the small of my back, at first I flinched from the unexpected sensation. But after she began softly pressing her thumbs and fingers into my muscles, I slowly relaxed, flitting my eyes in sublime bliss. Normally, I closed my eyes when I got a massage, concentrating on the relaxing feeling of my masseuse's fingers kneading my body. But with Hannah lying right next to me being serviced by a gorgeous Amazon, I kept them wide open, following her every movement and muscle twitch.

As she pressed her fingers into Hannah's back and slid her hands up and down her spine, I watched her tits jiggling and the muscles in her arms and stomach flexing. Her lower body was partially obscured by Hannah's prone figure, but that didn't stop me from dreaming about slipping my fingers into her bare snatch and licking her like a puppy dog. When the girls moved around to opposite sides of our tables revealing their bare asses for both of us to see, Hannah and I looked at one another again with wide eyes.

As I watched the front of my masseuse's body tensing and flexing only inches away from me, it took every ounce of my willpower not to reach out from the side of my table and touch her bald pussy. The more she caressed me, the more worked up I got watching the two girls' asses wiggling mere inches apart, and my hips began to squirm atop the rolled towel pressing into my pubis.

Just when I thought I couldn't take it any longer, the two masseuses moved to the other end of our bodies and began pressing their fingers into our calves, slowly working their way up our legs along the insides of our thighs. When the blonde girl reached the base of my buttocks, she stopped just short of my dripping slit then rolled her hands over my buttocks, squeezing them firmly. I pressed my mound down hard on the bumpy towel, desperately trying to give my aching clit some direct friction.

Feeling my buttocks flexing in her hands and sensing my rising tension, she swept her hands around the sides of my ass, cupping my cheeks with her thumbs pointed toward my fluttering pussy. I spread my legs further apart, inviting her to move her hand closer, and I gasped when she began running her thumbs up and down the sides of my slippery folds.

God yes, I thought, feeling my heart beginning to pound in my chest. *That's where I need your touch right now.*

I glanced over at Hannah, who had an equally intense look on her face as her attendant leaned over, caressing her vulva. I could see the slit of her masseuse's pussy between her round globes, and my eyes darted back and forth between the view of the blonde's bare mound moving inches away from my face and the brunette's inviting pussy glistening in the bright light of the massage room on the other side of Hannah's table.

I peered over at Hannah with my mouth agape and whispered *Thank You*. She simply smiled back at me and nodded knowingly. Something told me she knew exactly what she'd gotten us into, but at this precise moment I couldn't care less about her devious plan. Suddenly, the blonde girl adjusted her position with her left hand rested atop the base of my spine, while her other hand curled under my cheeks, penetrating my hole. When I felt her fingers enter my tunnel, I groaned, tilting my ass higher in the air.

Now I knew what the rolled-up towel was intended for. It was obviously meant to give the masseuses easier access to our undercarriage for this express purpose. As I began to roll my hips in concert with the blonde's probing of my pussy, I felt a stream of oil drip onto my buttocks, flowing down the crack of my ass over my rosebud and her dripping hand, now firmly embedded in my cunt. When I felt her other hand slide down over my ass and begin to massage my pucker, I groaned loudly and closed my eyes.

I was no longer interested in seeing what the other girl was doing to Hannah. I just wanted to concentrate on the heavenly sensation being administered by my own masseuse. When she began flicking my clit with the two little fingers of her right hand while she stimulated the walls of my pussy with her other fingers, I couldn't contain my pleasure any longer.

"Oh God," I moaned, fucking her hands with my ass and my pussy. My entire perineum from my asshole down to my clit was being simultaneously stimulated by the most sexy woman I'd seen in a long time.

"Yes," I purred, opening my eyes to see Hannah equally glazed over as her masseuse ministered to her in a similar manner.

I wondered if the couples' massage was designed to provide each of us simultaneous attention so we could arc through our pleasure in tandem. But at this point I hardly cared, as I surrendered to the mounting pleasure building inside me. Hannah and I peered at each other's faces while we read our bodies, knowing exactly what was happening to each other as we watched our reactions. We raised our arms over our heads and gripped the top of our padded tables tightly with our hands, and our mouths began to gape open as a flush rolled over each of our cheeks.

"Oh fuck," I groaned, feeling my orgasm beginning to pulse through me as my whole body began to shake. As I began clamping down on the blonde's fingers inside my pussy, she slipped her oiled thumb into my pucker while she fucked both of my holes as I writhed in delirious pleasure on the massage table.

"Uhnnn," Hannah groaned as I watched her ass quivering in the throes of her own powerful climax. The sight of the two gorgeous masseuse's fucking us with both hands while their bodies tensed and writhed overtop of our prone bodies was the most erotic thing I'd experienced in ages.

Hannah and I trembled and moaned on the massage tables for what seemed like an eternity, then our bodies both fell limp as our climaxes receded. For the first time in a long time, I felt completely relaxed and satisfied.

Maybe this spa idea wasn't such a bad idea after all, I smiled toward Hannah lying on the table next to me.

3

———————

After Hannah and I recovered from our dual massages, we headed to the pool to relax. The view of the city from the rooftop patio was magnificent, but the view *inside* was even more heart-stopping. Scores of naked women paraded in and out of the pool, while another group giggled inside an oversize, bubbling Jacuzzi. With the glass roof retracted, the bright overhead sun reflected off their glistening skin like sequins on their bare bodies.

We found two lounge chairs facing the shallow end of the pool and lay our bath towels on the padded cushions, then propped up the seatbacks so we'd have a good view of the action. The shallow end had descending steps leading into the basin, so we had a front-row seat for viewing the women as they slunk in and out of the water. As I watched the procession of beauties emerging from the pool dripping in erotic sensuality, I squeezed my thighs together trying to quiet my burning clit.

"You weren't kidding about this place being a voyeur's paradise," I chuckled to Hannah.

"Tell me about it," she said. "I can't decide if I prefer them coming or going."

"I could come again watching them either way. Is *everybody* in this place drop-dead gorgeous with model-perfect figures?"

"Well, it *is* the city's most exclusive spa, so I guess these girls know how to take care of themselves. But I also suspect a lot of it has to do with the fact that they know they're going to be under a microscope traipsing around in the nude. Maybe only the prettiest ones feel confident enough to flaunt their bodies so openly."

"Don't get me wrong," I said. "I'm definitely enjoying the show. It's just that I haven't felt this self-conscious about my body in a long time."

Hannah cocked her head toward me, peering over the top of her sunglasses.

"Don't sell yourself short, girl. You're just as pretty and sexy as any one of these hot mamas. Maybe you should get out there and do a little flaunting of your own."

"Perhaps in a little while," I said. "Right now, I'm just happy to do the watching."

"So are you glad I twisted your arm to come up here?" she said, lying back in her chair to soak up the sun.

"Definitely. This is even more dreamy than I imagined."

"And did you enjoy your massage?"

"Couldn't you tell? I think my masseuse probed every one of my erogenous zones."

"That's what I call a *full-body* massage," Hannah smiled.

"I was kind of hoping they'd flip us over afterward and get on top of us to complete the procedure. I don't know about you, but I had a hard time resisting the temptation to reach out and grope them as they moved around the table."

"I suspect that was all by design," Hannah nodded. "To build up our excitement for the big finish."

"That was a hell of a happy ending. I haven't come that hard in months."

"And we're just getting started," Hannah smiled. "Think of all the opportunities to connect in this place."

Suddenly, I noticed the pretty black girl from the locker room emerge from the outside patio and begin to walk in our direction.

"Oh, I'm *thinking*, alright," I said, pushing myself higher in my chair to get a better view.

Hannah followed my line of sight toward the girl and smiled.

"Isn't that the same girl you were eyeballing in the change room? She seems to be just as interested in you as you were in her."

As she moved closer toward us, we made eye contact, checking each other's figures out.

"I dunno, Han," I said. "I think she's out of my league. She looks like an African goddess."

"Well it appears that she's going to give us a bird's-eye view of her figure at least. Maybe she'll take a dip in the pool, where we can get a closer look at her."

As the girl walked toward the shallow end of the pool, I watched her tits jiggling on her chest and her long leg muscles flexing. When she got within a few feet of us, she turned toward the turquoise water and paused at the top of the steps. Her backside was even more spectacular than her front, with her swelling hips and a perfectly round ass accentuating her tawny, hourglass figure.

"Fuck me," I whispered to Hannah, peering down the crack of her ass toward the dark folds showing between her slightly parted thighs.

"That could be arranged if you play your cards right," she chuckled.

After a few seconds, the girl stepped into the water, slowly immersing her body into the sparkling surf. Then she leaned forward and began swimming toward the other end using a graceful breast stroke. As her legs flapped in and out, I watched her sexy ass rising and falling under the surface while the water swirled over her caramel body.

"Oh my God," I panted. "*Pinch* me to make sure I'm not dreaming."

"It's not a dream, babe," Hannah smiled. "That is one sexy-ass, flesh-and-blood woman."

"Just when I thought it couldn't possibly get any hotter than those two masseuses that worked us over. I'd take *this* one over three of them in a heartbeat."

When the girl reached the other end of the pool, she flipped over onto her other side and began swimming with a backstroke toward us. While her arms slowly windmilled through the water, her body rolled from side to side as the water washed over her sensuous breasts like waves on a beach. The closer she got to me, the more my heart raced, imagining her swimming right into my moistening lap.

"Yes, sweetheart," I purred, spreading my legs apart. "Dock yourself right here."

Hannah and I sat mesmerized watching her sylphlike figure slicing through the water, until one of her hands tapped the steps in the shallow end. Then she turned around and walked out of the water directly in front of us, smiling as she made eye contact with me. I couldn't help running my eyes over the front of her dripping body as my legs twitched involuntarily. Then she turned and retraced her steps around the perimeter of the pool, reclining in a vacant lounge chair at the opposite end.

"Did you see how she looked at you?" Hannah said, peering over at me. "She was practically fucking you with her eyes."

"I hardly noticed, watching the rest of her incredible body."

"I think you need to take advantage of this opportunity while the iron is still hot," she said. "Why don't you go over there and introduce yourself?"

"I wouldn't exactly say that was a green light to go hit on her. I don't want to intrude on her privacy if she just wants some peace and quiet."

"Well then, why don't you give her some of her own medicine by parading your body up and down the pool for everyone else to see? Let's see if she takes the bait."

"I don't know if *bait* is the right metaphor in this case, but I'd be thrilled if she gobbled me up right about now. I could use a refreshing dip in the pool anyways. After that hot massage session and watching that nymph take a sexy bath, I need to cool off. Hold my chair for me?"

"I wouldn't dream of giving it away. You go girl, go get your Lorelei."

I raised myself up from my chair then walked up to the edge of the shallow end and paused, peering across the reflecting surface hoping to catch the girl watching me from the other end of the pool. Although I was a little more full-figured than her, I maintained a tight, yoga-toned physique, with full, perky breasts, a flat stomach, and curvy hips. My pussy throbbed at the thought of her ogling me as I had with her.

While I lowered myself into the water, I kept my gaze pointed down, pretending to ignore her. Mimicking her lead, I began swimming breast strokes in her direction, with my head bobbing in and out of the water. When I neared the far wall, I glanced up at her chair resting near the edge of the pool and noticed her legs were slightly parted and she had a sexy smile on her face.

Jesus, I thought, touching the wall right in front of her. *Was she signaling her interest in me the same way I had earlier?*

As I turned around, I couldn't help smiling at our sexy cat-and-mouse game, then I pushed back from the wall floating on my back, using a reverse breast stroke technique. While I flapped my legs slowly in and out, I lifted my ass to the surface of the water, letting her watch the churning surf rising and falling over my exposed bare pussy. As I swung my arms slowly behind me, I glanced at the side of the pool and noticed that all the women were staring at my breasts poking out of the water.

Good, I thought. *Maybe if the African-American girl sees that I'm attracting the attention of some of the other pretty women, she'll make the next move.*

When I reached the shallow end, I walked up the stairs slowly so the girl on the other end could watch my round ass dripping with moisture. Then I lay down on my lounge chair next to Hannah, not even bothering to dry off.

"Holy shit, girl," she said. "I think you might have just one-upped your African goddess. Every set of eyes in the room was watching you as you swam across both lengths of the pool. You even got *me* going with that performance. If that doesn't pull her toward you like a magnet, I don't know what will."

I turned my head to gaze in the black girl's direction and noticed she was walking back toward our end once again.

"See?" Hannah said. "You've obviously tweaked her interest. Let's see if she says hello."

As the girl moved closer toward us, I could feel my pussy throbbing, but when she reached the end of the pool, she glimpsed at me briefly then continued on to the end of the platform, disappearing into the sauna room.

"*Well?*" Hannah said, peering at me with raised eyebrows. "What are you waiting for? That's an invitation if I ever saw one."

"Yeah?" I said, still not convinced. "Are you sure?"

"She was watching you the entire walk back toward our end of the pool. Then she goes into a private room in full view of you. I don't think you need a crystal ball to know that she wants you."

"Okay," I said. "Should I bring a towel or something to cover up?"

"Was *she* wearing a towel?" Hannah said sarcastically.

"Fine. But if I'm not out in twenty minutes, come check up on me to make sure I haven't passed out or something. I'm feeling so light-headed right now, I'm afraid all that hot steam might make me collapse at the knees."

"I'm quite sure you won't need any help from me," she said. "But if she happens to come out first and I don't see any sign of you within a few minutes, I'll make sure you haven't fainted from all the pleasure you're about to receive."

"Wish me luck," I said, slowly rising from my chair, trying not to make it too obvious to everybody else in the room that I was following the girl into the sauna.

When I got to the room, I swung open the door and saw her sitting on the upper bunk with her left knee propped up on the bench, exposing her pink slit. Another woman rested on the bench directly beneath her, leaning back against the wood planks with her hands resting by her sides. I took a position kitty-corner to them on the lower bench, then leaned back against the wall with my opposite leg propped up, concealing my pussy.

I lay my head back and closed my eyes, pretending to relax and enjoy the hot steam. But when I opened them briefly and peered in the black girl's direction, I saw her right hand positioned in front of her pussy, moving her fingers in slow circles below her mound.

Holy shit, I thought. *She's playing with herself in full view of me!*

At first, I was so shocked at her brazen act of exhibitionism that I looked away, thinking she wanted to watch me only when she knew I wasn't looking. But when I peered back at her a few moments later, her legs were spread even further apart, exposing her beautiful pink vulva against her chocolate-brown skin. As her hand began to move in faster circles over her clit, her mouth parted open and I could hear her panting softly.

I glanced down at the other woman sitting below her who still had her eyes closed, oblivious to the ministrations of the sexy girl sitting directly above her. Feeling the sticky juices building up between my legs, I lowered my right hand into my lap and began rubbing my clit behind my propped-up leg. I didn't feel comfortable exposing myself fully in case the other woman opened her eyes, but I gazed directly back at the black girl as we massaged our clits.

As I began to feel the sweat dripping over my forehead and the pleasure spreading throughout my body, I slowly lowered my raised leg and spread my thighs apart, showing the girl my dripping pussy. She grabbed one of her tits with her free hand and pinched her long nipple while she stared at my glistening snatch. Before long, both of us were moaning softly, jilling ourselves with increasing fervor.

When I glanced down at the other woman to make sure it was still safe, I was surprised to see that she also had her legs spread apart and was rubbing her pussy as she watched me playing with myself. But at this point, I was too far gone to stop what I was doing, and knowing that the we were all aligned with our intentions, I began to moan and twist my hips on the warm cedar bench. When the black girl thrust her hand inside her pink folds and began thumping her back against the wall in rising pleasure, I couldn't resist the temptation any longer.

I rose from my bench and walked directly in front of her, positioning my head between her legs, then I pulled her hips hard into my face, eating her pussy like it was my last meal. She placed her hands behind my head and pulled me toward her, squeezing my head between her powerful thighs. As I reached up to grab her tits, I felt the woman's hand from below probing my slit, then she placed two fingers thrust inside me. While I moaned into the black girl's cunt, I lifted one foot and placed it on the bench beside the other woman and I felt her lips suck my erect clit into her mouth.

With my face buried in the black girl's snatch and my own pussy being serviced from below, I moaned into her cleft, feeling my orgasm approaching like a freight train. When it slammed into me, I groaned loudly into the girl's pussy, and she grabbed my hair while she clamped her thighs tightly against the sides of my head, quivering on the edge of the bench.

She held me in this clenched position for so long I was afraid she might suffocate me, but I dared not come up for air while she was in the throes of a powerful orgasm. After many long seconds, she finally loosened her grip and relaxed her legs then she leaned forward, thrusting her tongue into my dripping mouth. As we kissed each other passionately, the woman below removed her fingers from my pussy and I heard the sound of her breathing beginning to escalate while she attended to her own needs.

For the entire time the three of us were in the sauna, none of us had said a single word to one another. I didn't even know the *name* of the girl whose cunt I'd just finished eating out. There was something about this anonymous, no-strings-attached, down-and-dirty spa that I was digging. It didn't look like Hannah would have to save me after all.

For the first time since entering the spa, I felt completely liberated, ready to explore all the carnal opportunities on my own.

4

———————

Feeling a bit awkward after my fling in the sauna, I left the room soon after and headed back over to my spot by the pool. I saw Hannah taking a leisurely swim, so I headed over to the juice bar and picked up two smoothies. When I returned to my lounge chair, I glanced around the room, soaking up the scene. With so many sexy women prancing around the place, I was surprised more of them weren't hooking up.

Maybe they're just self-conscious about making out in public, I thought. *Or maybe they're waiting for someone to break the ice.*

I glanced over in the direction of the hot tub, noticing a small group of women chatting and laughing in the bubbly froth.

If that's not the perfect place for a little extra-curricular activity, I don't know what is.

Hannah emerged from the pool and walked toward me, wringing out her hair.

"*So?*" she smiled. "How did it go in there? Did you finally get your freak on with your African goddess?"

"It definitely got pretty hot," I nodded.

"Like, almost *pass-out* hot? I'm a little disappointed you didn't call for reinforcements. Try as I might to attract the attention of other women in this place, everybody seems to be ignoring me."

I glanced at Hannah's naked body, admiring her tight, shapely figure. There was no reason she shouldn't be connecting with other girls, and I felt a little guilty for abandoning her.

"Maybe you just need a little extra *lubricant*," I said. "The hot tub in the corner looks like it might be more conducive for some close-quarter mingling. Do you want to give it a go?"

"Sure," Hannah said. "But don't you need a little time to recover? What happened to your girlfriend?"

"It seems she was only interested in one thing," I shrugged. "But I *could* use a little rest."

I pointed to the tall glass resting on the table beside Hannah's chair.

"I brought you a smoothie. Why don't we cool off before jumping back into the fire?"

Hannah patted her hair dry with a towel then lay back in her chair, taking a sip of her smoothie.

"So, have you had your eye on anyone *else* in this place?"

"Not really," I said. "Just about everybody looks seriously fuckable. I wouldn't mind wrapping my legs around that cute blonde masseuse though, if I had a chance. But I'm guessing that's against the rules."

"I dunno. What's good for the goose is good for the gander, in a manner of speaking. Maybe you just need to get her alone someplace."

"Perhaps I can schedule a *one-on-one* massage next time," I said. "I'm pretty sure I could persuade her to participate in a more interactive session if I had her all to myself."

"So you're thinking of coming *back*, then?" Hannah smiled. "Have they got you hooked already?"

"It's pretty hard to ignore a place like this," I nodded. "I wonder if they have monthly memberships?"

"The amenities would seem to fit that model. It's almost like more of a *health club*, with a few extra perks. Albeit some pretty fucking *awesome* perks."

"Speaking of," I said, peering over in the direction of the girls in the hot tub. "Are you ready to check out some of those other amenities?"

"Absolutely," she smiled. "If I can't hook up with someone there, at least I should be able to get some *other* kind of stimulation in the Jacuzzi."

We picked up our unfinished smoothies and carried them over toward the hot tub. When we got there, I noticed there were already four women submerged in the bubbling water and I wondered if there'd be enough room for Hannah and me.

"Have you got room for two more?" I asked.

"Absolutely," one of the girls said. "The more the merrier."

The women pressed their bodies closer together, and Hannah and I scooched in next to them. The water was warmer than I expected, but it didn't take long for me to get used to it, especially with the fleshy bodies of the other women rubbing up next to me.

"I haven't seen you guys here before," a forty-something redhead said, smiling at me. "First time visiting our spa?"

"Yes," I said.

"What do you think so far?"

"It's definitely a different kind of experience," I nodded, not yet ready to reveal just how *much* I'd actually enjoyed it.

"Have you availed yourself of any of the special services yet?" she said.

"Hannah and I had a couples massage a little while ago. It was very invigorating."

"Yes, those masseuses really know how to pinpoint the right spots," she smiled. "I'm Amber by the way."

I scanned her pretty face, admiring her piercing green eyes and high cheekbones. Although she was slightly older than most of the other women in the spa, she was equally as stunning, reminding me of the pretty runway model, Angie Everhart.

"Jade," I said. "And this is–"

"Hannah," Amber nodded. "Nice to see some fresh meat in this place, what do you think girls?" She peered around her, nodding at the other women in the tub, roughly her same age. "This is Kat, Anna, and Tammy."

"So are you guys–" I said, wondering if they came here often.

"Old fogies?" Amber laughed. "Yeah, I guess you could say we're regulars. There's more than *one* way to stay young at heart, you know."

"Speaking of," her friend Kat smiled. "We noticed you and that pretty black girl checking each other out earlier. Were you finally able to consummate your little courtship in the sauna?"

"Um..."

"It's okay," Amber chuckled. "We know *everything* that goes on in this place. Why else would we have lifetime memberships?"

I huffed softly, not quite sure how to respond.

"So are you two–?" Amber said, glancing at Hannah.

"No," Hannah said, shaking her head. "We're just good friends."

"That's a shame, because you look like a perfect match. Two pretty girls, one a blonde, the other a brunette. What are you, like barely *thirty*?"

"That's very generous," Hannah chuckled. "Just a little north of that. Maybe this invigorating spa treatment is beginning to work it's wonders already."

"There's a good chance. But you look like you could use a little extra stimulation. While your girlfriend's been improving her circulation in the steam room, you've been left to your own devices. There's a special spot over here where you can have some extra fun if you want."

"Oh?" Hannah said, suddenly perking up.

"I've been sitting right in front of it this whole time. Would you like to give it a try?"

"Sure," Hannah said, happy to have attracted the attention of some other women finally.

"Come," Amber said, standing up in the pool. "Let's switch positions. You come sit over here next to Kat and I'll sit next to your pretty girlfriend."

While Hannah and Amber switched positions, I took a moment

to check out Amber's body. She had plump breasts with surprising firmness for her age and well-toned arms with tight, supple skin. Her wet hair draped over her lightly speckled chest and with her flushed cheeks and erect nipples, I found myself unconsciously spreading my legs trying to increase the flow of swirling water over my throbbing pussy.

When Hannah sat in her vacated spot, Kat suddenly reached under the water, pulling her legs forward a few inches, and Hannah's face lit up.

"*Right?*" Amber smiled, pressing her body up next to me. "I told you you'd like it. There's nothing like an invigorating water jet massage directed to the perfect location. Are you feeling more comfortable now?"

"Oh *yes*," Hannah grunted, shifting her hips closer to the pulsating underwater stream. "This is way better than the usual sex toys I'm accustomed to."

"And the best part is there's no *cleanup* required afterward. You can get off and freshen up at the same time."

"Mmm," Hannah moaned, surrendering to the feeling of the powerful spray stimulating her clit.

Suddenly Kat turned her body toward her and reached under the water, caressing her tits.

"Uhnn," Hannah groaned, turning her face toward Kat as they began kissing.

"Now *that's* a beautiful sight, don't you agree, Jade?"

"Absolutely," I hummed. "This is just what Hannah needed."

Amber placed her hand under the water and extended her arm toward my crotch. When she felt my fingers moving softly over my clit, she lowered her hand a few inches lower, thrusting two fingers into my hole. I didn't know what it was about this place, but I didn't seem to mind the members taking these kinds of liberties with my body. Between the swirling water jets pounding against my hips and Amber's sexy body rubbing up against my breasts, I was more than ready to ramp things up.

"That's a nice tight cunny you have," Amber purred. "Shall I continue?"

"Yes please," I moaned, flitting my eyelids in pleasure.

Amber suddenly raised herself off the bench and turned around to face me, straddling my hips and pressing her mound into my stomach.

"Mmm," she purred, pressing her melons against my tits. "You're *soft*, too. Do you like watching your girlfriend getting off under the water?"

"Yes," I panted.

With the four of us now actively engaged with each other, Tammy raised herself off her seat and sat down over Anna's thighs, facing the rest of us. Apparently, nobody except Amber wanted to miss catching the rest of the action in the hot tub while we groped and caressed one another.

Amber reached behind her back with her hand, cupping my trembling hand as I massaged my pussy. Then she placed three fingers inside me, fucking me while I stimulated my clit. She leaned in to kiss me, and I felt her hips tilt as she began rocking her pussy against the top of my mound. The idea of being fucked by this sexy older redhead while she rubbed her big tits against my breasts excited me tremendously, and before long we were tongue-fucking each other as we moaned into each other's mouths.

I peered over at Anna and Tammy, whose eyes were glazed over watching the rest of us as they rubbed their vulvas together with Anna squeezing her friend's tits from behind. Then I glanced over at Hannah and saw that Kat had angled her body toward her with one leg resting over her thigh, trying to get in on the powerful stream now pulsing toward both of their pussies. She smiled at me, nodding at how pleased she was with the turn of events.

With the heat in the hot tub beginning to ramp up, Amber and I began pressing our hips together more vigorously as our moans began rising in pitch in volume, and I could feel myself veering on the precipice, ready to pop off any second. Sensing I was close, Amber pressed her palm harder against my fluttering hand while she stroked my G-spot with her three fingers. Then she pressed her little finger further down my perineum until it rested against my pucker. While she moved her hand in circles overtop of mine, I spread my legs further apart, moaning loudly into her mouth.

"Yes," I grunted, feeling myself falling over the edge. "You're going to make me cum, Amber. *Oh my God–*"

As my orgasm washed over me, Amber pressed her little finger into my rosebud, and my entire perineum began clamping down over her hand.

"Yes, baby," she purred. "Let it go. Come for Momma."

I could feel her press her pussy more forcefully into my stomach as she rocked her hips with greater urgency, gripping my hips with her thighs.

"Uhnnn!" I cried, consumed with pleasure as I watched the other girls reaching their apex at the same time.

When the six of us finally stopping grunting and groaning, I looked around the spa and noticed that virtually everybody else in the poolroom had suddenly paired up, enjoying their own little moment of bliss.

5

____

After the wild ride in the hot tub, I needed some alone time, so I headed to the exercise studio to stretch and relax. Finding it empty, I walked over to a large padded mat against the far wall and sat down, pulling my hands toward my feet to loosen my leg muscles. The entire room was lined in floor-to-ceiling mirrors, with equal parts dedicated to aerobic classes, weight machines, and stretching. I remembered seeing aerobic classes on the list of services at the front desk, and I smiled at the thought of everybody's boobs bouncing up and down as they went through their paces.

No wonder everyone in this place is so fit and toned, I thought. There weren't many places in the spa where you could avoid being seen or seeing your own naked body from just about any angle. *There's virtually nowhere to hide or cover up.*

As I moved through my usual yoga poses on the mat, I watched myself in the mirror. I was proud of the tight figure I'd been able to maintain over the years, and I smiled seeing the muscles flexing in my arms and legs while I strained to hold the poses. But stretching in the buff was a whole *different* experience, and I felt my nipples hardening and my pussy moistening as I watched my tits and glistening vulva in the glass.

While I held my toes high off the mat balancing on my ass in a split-leg position, suddenly the door swung open and a familiar face entered the room. It was the pretty blonde from the massage room. She glanced at my exposed pussy reflecting in the mirror and smiled when I lowered my feet, closing my legs to protect my modesty.

"Don't stop on my account," she said, taking a position on the mat a few feet to my side. "A woman with your physique shouldn't be afraid to reveal every part of her glorious figure."

"Thanks," I said, leaning forward to rest my breasts on top of my thighs. "I didn't want to be too bold. I already feel exposed enough in this place as it is."

"You shouldn't feel self-conscious in here," she said. "That's the beauty of this spa. It's a place where women can go to free their minds and spirits without feeling judged in any way."

"It seems that's not the *only* thing that gets freed in this place," I smiled, alluding to our intimate session earlier in the day. "I had no idea I'd be releasing my inhibitions in so many different ways."

"*Jade*, isn't it?" she said, pinching her eyebrows together. "I remember you from this morning's massage."

"Yes," I said, blushing softly.

"I'm Julie," she said, reaching out to extend her hand. "We were never properly introduced."

"No, I suppose not," I said, feeling the hairs on my arms standing on end as I touched her for the first time. "I guess we were too preoccupied with other things."

"Mmm," she nodded. "Have you enjoyed your visit to our spa so far?"

"Oh yes," I said. "It's far surpassed my expectations. It's been a feast for the senses in so many ways. So much so that I needed to come in here and wind down for a few moments."

"I know what you mean," Julie said. "I like to come in here to stretch and meditate between appointments. I find it very therapeutic."

I watched her in the mirror as she twisted and contorted her body into increasingly difficult poses.

"How long have you been working here?"

"Only a couple of months. It's nice that the management allows us to use the facilities along with the rest of the members and guests."

As she moved through her stretches and poses, I marveled at her tight, lithesome figure. She was more slender than me, with smaller but firmer breasts and long, sinewy muscles that flexed sensuously as she went through her motions. When she leaned forward and lifted herself off the mat into a crow position, I admired her flexing arm muscles supporting her weight. But when she shifted into an inverted arm balance with her legs curved up over her shoulders, I couldn't help peering between her legs at her exposed slit.

"I always found that pose one of the tougher ones to hold," I said, feeling my pussy growing wetter by the moment.

"The key is to place your arms far enough apart with your legs positioned forward," she said. "Then slowly tilt your weight until you feel yourself balanced on your hands. Why don't you try it with me?"

She dropped her legs to the floor, then placed her hands and feet on the mat in a bent-over pose.

"You start in this position then gradually shift more of your weight over your hands. When you feel like you're supporting most of your weight on your arms, curl your legs forward and raise your feet off the floor."

I followed Julie's lead, panting heavily as I strained my arm muscles trying to support my weight.

"That's it," she nodded, seeing me raise my ass off the floor. "Now cross your ankles in front of your arms to lock yourself into position."

When I finally achieved the position, it felt surprisingly easy to hold the pose with everything held neatly together.

"That's excellent," Julie smiled. "It's not so difficult when you get into the right position, is it?"

"No," I puffed, staring at her pretty tits pressing together in the bent-over pose.

"Do you want to try something a little more challenging?" she asked.

"Okay," I said, feeling the cool air from below flowing over my exposed pussy.

"Keep your weight balanced over your arms, then unlock your ankles and extend your legs straight out in front of you until they're parallel with the floor."

I followed Julie's direction, grunting loudly as I felt the pressure building on my arms.

"Remember to keep your weight shifted forward so you don't fall back."

After a few seconds of struggling, I managed to achieve the pose, albeit with slightly crooked legs.

"That's fantastic, Jade," Julie said, peering at me in the mirror. "Why don't we take it one step further and see if we can shift into the firefly position."

Julie angled her legs higher in the air, tilting her ass toward the floor until her legs were pointed forty-five degrees up in the air, with her entire body balancing on her outstretched arms. With her pussy staring directly in front of me between her splayed legs, it took all of my concentration to stay focused on executing the technique.

"I'll try," I panted, feeling some drops of lubrication falling onto the mat between my legs.

With my legs pointing forward as much as I could, I slowly lowered my hips toward the floor, balancing my suspended weight over my arms until I matched the angle of Julie's upturned legs. I could feel the strain in my hamstrings from my legs pulled back behind my shoulders, and I glanced in the mirror, seeing the reflection of the bright overhead lights reflecting off my glistening, wet pussy.

"You got it, girl!" Julie said, peering between my legs. "How does it feel?"

"Strangely invigorating," I grunted, running my eyes all over Julie's body in front of me. "But this is killing my hamstrings. I think I need to loosen up a bit more before trying some of these more advanced poses."

"Absolutely," she nodded. "You don't want to hurt yourself. Let's give your muscles a rest before you pull something."

I lowered myself onto the mat then placed my hands beside my quivering legs, breathing heavily in and out.

"That was exhilarating," I said, peering over at Julie. "You've obviously got many talents beyond massage therapy."

"It's all part of the mind-body connection," she smiled. "Strength, flexibility, relaxation. It keeps us healthy in many different ways."

I glanced at her perfect tits glistening with sweat, feeling my pussy throbbing in excitement.

"If this is what it takes to achieve your level of fitness, I'm all in. I don't think I've seen another woman with as perfectly toned a figure as yours."

"You're no slouch yourself, Jade. It's just a matter of building up your stamina. Do you want to try some *partnered* stretching to loosen up your muscles a bit more?"

I'd been waiting for a chance to pair up with the pretty masseuse, and when she indicated she was ready to move to a new phase in our routine, I suddenly became aware of the puddle forming on the mat between my legs.

"As long as you promise not to twist me into a pretzel this time."

"No worries," she smiled. "This next one is super simple and far more relaxing. All you have to do is sit on the mat with your legs extended in front of you, with your feet spread apart a few inches. I'll face towards you with our feet touching together, then we can hold hands and gently pull each other forward and back to stretch the back of our leg muscles."

I nodded, imagining myself rocking back and forth with her in whole *different* kind of position.

Julie shifted her body around in front of me, and when she spread her legs and touched her feet to mine, I felt a surge of electricity coursing through me. I had to fight hard to keep my gaze above her neckline as she smiled and reached out her hands toward me.

"Now bend forward one inch at a time while I hold your arms. When you feel the tension in the back of your thighs, breathe deeply and try to relax until you feel the pressure receding."

I was able to bend forward far enough to clasp her hands, and I smiled when she squeezed me gently.

"Now, let me pull you slowly toward me until you feel tightness in your hamstrings again. Stop me when it begins to bind, then breathe slowly in and out until you feel your leg muscles relax."

I did as she instructed, and after a few minutes Julie was able to pull my upper body almost parallel with my legs resting on the floor.

"There you go," she nodded. "Now let's see if we can do the same thing with the adductor muscles on the inside of your thighs. I want you to spread your feet slowly apart as I maintain tension on your arms. You should feel pressure in the muscles on the side of your crotch as you begin to lengthen the tendons on the inside of your legs."

"I definitely feel *something* there," I huffed, watching the slit between Julie's legs open wider and wider the further I pressed my legs apart. She glanced between my thighs, noticing the wet spot on the mat directly in front of me.

"Remember to go slow," she said. "You definitely don't want to pull *this* muscle. This one's pretty important for maintaining sexual health and flexibility."

"You don't have to remind me twice about that one," I smiled. "I definitely don't want to put a damper on that."

"Okay, now lean back and begin to pull *me* forward now. This way we can *both* benefit from this stretch while we pump the blood through our muscles in this area."

"Yes," I purred, pulling her upper body toward me as we pressed our feet further apart. "I feel my circulation improving already."

The more we pulled our bodies toward one another, the further our legs pressed apart, bringing our pussies closer together and our bodies closer to touching. But just as her face moved to within inches of my throbbing snatch, the gym door swung open and two women paused at the entrance, seeing us in the compromising position.

"Do you mind if we join you?" one of the girls said, staring at the glistening reflection of my wet pussy.

"I'm good if you are, Jade," Julie said while I felt her breath inches away from my dripping pussy.

"Of course," I said, not wanting to throw a wet blanket on our fun. "There's lots of room on the mat for more people."

The girls sat down beside us, assuming a similar position.

"That stretch looks interesting," the first one said. "It certainly looks more stimulating than doing it alone."

"It's even more fun to perform it as a *group*," Julie said. "Why don't we form a circle with our feet touching and see if we can stretch and loosen our muscles *together*?"

She shifted her ass back a few inches then spread her legs further apart, inviting the girls into the circle. They positioned themselves next to us, then Julie spread her arm to her side, clasping the hand of the girl next to her. I did the same until we were all holding hands with our legs forty-five degrees apart, touching our feet in a chain-link circle.

"Well now that we're getting to know each other a little better," the first girl said. "I suppose we should introduce ourselves. I'm Taylor and this is Quinn."

"Pleased to meet you," Julie said. "I'm Julie."

"Jade," I said, nodding to each of the girls.

"So how does this work exactly?" Taylor said, glancing down at the juices coating the inside of my thighs.

"Jade and I were pulling each other to stretch our hamstrings and adductor muscles. But in a perfect circle, we'll be maintaining equal pressure between the four of us, so in order to move closer together, let's try spreading our legs further apart."

As we all followed Julie's instructions, our circle slowly began collapsing into a diamond shape.

"That's the idea," Julie said. "Can you girls feel the tension between your legs the closer we get to one another?"

"Yes, and that's not the *only* thing I'm feeling," Quinn said, glancing at our glistening pussies coming closer together.

"When we get close enough to our partners," Julie said, "reach out and clasp her hands, pulling you closer together. As you rock back and forth, you should be able to spread your feet further apart, slowly releasing the tension on the inside of your thighs."

"Mmm," Taylor groaned. "I feel it. How close should we try to get to one another?"

"As close as possible," Julie smiled. "If you can relax your adductors enough, ideally you should be able to touch in the middle."

As the four of us pulled each other closer and closer, spreading our legs further apart, Julie's upper body began to bend over my hips with her tits edging tantalizingly close to my throbbing pussy. I glanced at Taylor and Quinn, whose feet were pressed against the sides of Julie's and mine, and they smiled at each other as they peered between each of their open legs. Before long, both couple's glistening pussies were only inches apart as we pulled our upper bodies closer toward our hardening nipples and parted mouths. When I felt the strands of Julie's hair caress the top of my breasts, I pulled her harder toward me and she encircled one of my teats in her mouth.

"Mmm," I groaned, trying to spread my legs into a one-hundred-and-eighty-degree split, desperate to feel her pussy up against me.

But after a few moments, she began pulling me in the opposite direction. As I leaned forward over her tight abdomen, I licked my tongue up the crease in the center of her stomach until I reached the base of her tits. Then I sucked her medallions into my mouth, circling her nipples with my tongue, and she tilted her hips forward, touching our vulvas. I moaned loudly into her breasts when I felt our juices intermingling, but as soon as our clits touched, she suddenly leaned forward, pressing her body back in my direction.

I was beginning to go crazy with all this reciprocal teasing, wanting to feel Julie's lips against my own as we ground our pussies together. By now, all four of us had our legs spread into a virtual split, with the original circle collapsed into two parallel lines. Growing impatient, I pulled Julie hard toward me until her body rested on top of me, and she began kissing me as we rubbed our tits and vulvas together. This time, there was no desire for either of one of us to separate while we ground our wet pussies together, rubbing our hard clits over one another.

"Fuck yes," I purred into her mouth. "This is insanely hot. Rub your body against me, Julie."

"You've reached the height of your flexibility," she nodded. "Now just try to relax your muscles while you let the rest of your body enjoy the experience."

"Oh yes," I panted. "I'm definitely shifting my concentration to *other* parts of my body."

I peered at Taylor and Quinn out of the corner of my eye and saw that they were similarly commingled, rubbing their pussies and tits against one another with their legs spread wide apart.

"Uhhn," I heard them groan next to Julie and me.

There was something incredibly sexy about the four of us touching our feet together while we rubbed our bodies next to one another, listening to the mounting passion generated between the four of us. I tilted my head up a few inches and looked in the mirror in front of us. With Julie's legs splayed wide apart and our mounds joined together, I saw both of our slits spread open as our juices rolled down over each other's vulvas. I'd never seen anything so sexy in all my life, and the fact that we were engaged in a two-way affair with Taylor and Quinn right next to us just added to my excitement.

I began to feel the pleasure rising inside me and with our hands no longer needed to pull ourselves together, I wrapped my arms around Julie's back and thrust my tongue into her mouth, feeling my climax edging closer. When it finally hit me, I groaned loudly in Julie's mouth, spraying my juices over her vulva and ass while she grunted simultaneously inside my mouth. As the four of us writhed and groaned on the mat in simultaneous union, I heard some movement by the door and glanced up to see a large group of women pausing at the entrance, with their mouths wide agape.

It didn't take long for them to rush toward us joining us on the mat, rolling together in a giant heap of naked, writing bodies. As we intertwined our arms and legs, sucking and rocking against whatever body part presented itself to each of us, I smiled realizing I'd reached a new kind of nirvana. Something told me this spa was about to become my new go-to gym for the foreseeable future.

MAID SERVICE

AN EROTIC ADVENTURE

1

I t had been a long week on the road, and I was beginning to feel a bit antsy. I'd never really enjoyed business travel. The days were usually long, and my nights were often spent preparing for the following day's meetings. Granted, my clients took me out for a nice dinner afterwards, but those too were tiring, as I had to keep my game face on trying to land another hard-fought commission.

Being a freelance graphic designer was a tough gig, and I was always mindful of the need to coddle my buyer while not appearing to oversell my services. The idea of using these getaways for a quick hookup with a new acquaintance was out of the question. Not only was I usually too tired at the end of the day, but I had to keep a professional distance with my business associates.

I'd gotten up early to prepare for an important presentation later in the day, and after rubbing out a quick orgasm and having a shower, I sat down in front of my laptop at the small desk in my hotel room. But after reviewing a few slides of my PowerPoint deck, I paused and stared at the screen. This was the least fun part of my job, and I shifted the cursor over the address bar of my browser, preparing to type in the URL for my favorite lesbian website. I was still buzzing from my morning play time, and my panties were already wet thinking about watching some hot girls tribbing their pussies together. Just as I was about to take off my clothes and make myself more comfortable, I heard a gentle tap on my door.

"Housekeeping," a soft voice called.

Normally I'd ask the maid to return later in the day when I wasn't so busy. But I was caught unprepared and hastily pulled my jeans up before responding.

"Um–just a moment, please," I stammered.

I looked in the mirror at the front of the table and straightened my hair, trying to compose myself.

"Come in," I said, feeling my heartbeat returning to normal.

The maid opened the door and wedged her cart in the entrance, then hesitated when she saw me working at the table. She was younger and prettier than I expected, with dark brown eyes, soft caramel-colored skin, and puffy rosebud lips. I took a quick scan of her curvy figure and sat upright in my chair.

"Don't mind me," I said, feeling my pussy twitch unconsciously. "I'm just getting caught up on some work. Do you mind if I finish up while you clean the room?"

"Of course," she said. "I'll just be a few minutes."

She grabbed some fresh linens from her cart and disappeared into the bathroom. As I listened to her hanging up the towels and wiping down the counter, I suddenly remembered that I'd left my used vibrator next to the sink. Horrified, I glanced up and saw her pushing it to the side of the table while she peered up at me in the mirror. I blushed a deep shade of crimson and returned my gaze to my computer, pretending to tap away at the keyboard.

What the fuck, Jade, I muttered to myself, shaking my head in dismay. *Couldn't you have hidden the damn thing before you left the washroom?*

The maid seemed to take longer than usual to wipe down the surface as she rearranged my toiletries into a neat pile at the corner of the sink. I always felt a bit peeved whenever the housekeeping staff moved my personal effects, but today I was more put off than usual. Recognizing more movement out of the corner of my eye, I turned once again to see her leaning over and wiggling her ass as she finished wiping down the countertop.

She was wearing a one-piece black dress with a buttoned-up white collar and a short apron tied around her shapely hips. As she bent over and cleaned the vanity, I watched the muscles in the back of her legs flex while she swayed her hips in little circles. She caught my gaze once again in the bathroom mirror and smiled at me demurely.

Fuck me, I thought. *Are all the maids in this place this hot?*

I returned my attention to my computer and banged away at the keyboard as a jumble of random characters filled my slide. At this point, I had no idea what was appearing on my screen while I fantasied about kneeling between the girl's legs and slurping her pussy from behind. I could feel the wet spot beginning to grow in my panties, and I shifted uncomfortably on my chair, trying to distract attention from my aching clit.

When she emerged from the washroom, I turned toward her and noticed that she'd placed my purple Rabbit vibrator standing up on the side of the counter next to my toothbrush. The simulated penis head and protruding rabbit ears on the shaft stared out at me, mocking me for my absent-minded oversight.

Jesus Christ, I thought. *I wonder what she made of the unusual dildo. Had she even seen one of those things before?*

The thought of her touching my sex toy got me even more worked up as I imagined her pleasuring herself with the multi-functional device. Of course, I couldn't say anything, let alone acknowledge that she'd actually *touched* the object that had throbbed inside my pussy only a few minutes earlier.

As she strode toward my unmade bed, I was tempted to tell her to leave it as it was, since I knew it was hotel policy not to replace the linens until the next guest arrived. There wasn't really any need to make it up, since no one else would be seeing it for the remainder of the day and I'd just be climbing back into it in a matter of hours. But as I watched her glide around the side of the bed, I was so mesmerized watching her body in the mirror, I felt paralyzed.

As she leaned over the edge of the mattress, pulling the sheets toward the headboard, I saw her side profile for the first time. Even though her dress was buttoned all the way up the front of her chest, I could clearly see the outline of her breasts against the background of the stark white linens. Her tits were long and pointed, with wide separation between each peak, like she was wearing an old-fashioned corset underneath her tight uniform. With her light brown hair pulled back in a bun behind her head, I studied every curve and contour of her pretty face. Her cheekbones were high and round like a native American, but her cheeks were carved like a supermodel's. With her golden-brown skin and smoldering eyes, she looked like a cross between Jessica Alba and Jennifer Lopez.

Oh my God, I drooled, staring at her in my mirror. *How has this angel not already been swooped up by some handsome billionaire and whisked away to his private enclave? Was this her first week on the job and still too naive to know that with that body and those looks, she could write her own ticket?*

As she smoothed down the sheets and wrapped them around the base of the mattress, I leered at her tight ass, fantasizing about all the ways I'd like to fuck her. By now, my panties were so soaked, I'd formed a large wet patch in the crotch of my pants, and I squeezed my thighs together, trying to quiet my raging clit.

When the girl swept around the base of the bed directly behind me, I smelled her perfume, as a light breeze wafted over my shoulders. It smelled sweet and flowery, just like I imagined her to be. I couldn't make out the brand, but I resolved right then and there to go to the nearest department store at my earliest opportunity to find it for myself. Even if it didn't suit me personally, I longed to feel her scent on my body while I fantasied about rubbing our bodies together.

When she shifted over to the other side of the bed to repeat the sequence, I angled my head in the mirror to watch her ass in the reflection of the large picture window overlooking the street. As she leaned over, she swung one of her legs up to support herself while she propped up the pillows in the middle of my oversize bed, and I caught a glimpse of the back of her thighs and a small patch of white cloth between her legs.

Oh, I moaned out loud, imagining what she'd look like completely naked. I wanted this sexy vixen, and I wanted her *now*. But short of jumping on top of her and pinning her to my bed, I was completely at her mercy while I watched her go about her duties. Besides, the door was still ajar, and we'd have no privacy if either one of us had any amorous ideas.

She rearranged the room service menu and placed a fresh bottle of water at the side of the table next to me, then peered up at me in the mirror and smiled.

"Was there anything else you needed, Madam?" she asked.

I paused for a long moment as the words stuck in my throat.

I wanted to tell her how much I wanted to make a mess of her newly remade bed while I wrapped my legs around her and plunged my tongue down her throat, but I shook my head and sighed.

"No," I said. "Thank you for everything. I'm good to go."

She nodded at me, then pushed her housekeeping cart over the threshold, softly closing the door behind her.

Good to go? I thought to myself. *What a lightweight you are, Jade. If you had any guts, you'd have taken her in your arms and kissed her like a proper lady.* After all, she'd given me plenty of clues that she was just as interested in me as I was with her.

As soon as I heard her move her cart to the next room and knock on the adjacent door, I leapt to my feet and grabbed my Rabbit vibrator off the bathroom countertop. Then I tore off my clothes and kneeled on my bed, facing the desk mirror. As I plunged the phallus deep into my dripping pussy and turned the setting to max, I dreamed it was the pretty maid who was staring back at me.

I still have three days to get you into my bed, I murmured. *One way or the other, I'll have you before this week is over.*

2

———

I was so fixated fantasizing about the pretty maid for the rest of the morning, I was late for my scheduled meeting with my client. When I got to the office, I could barely concentrate on my presentation, flashing back and forth between her exquisite ass and her Gina Lollobrigida tits. Everybody else in my sphere of influence suddenly seemed so dull and boring. When my buyer invited me for dinner that evening, I reluctantly agreed, knowing I'd have an even harder time concentrating as I dreamt about slipping back under my covers, smelling her intoxicating scent.

When I returned to my hotel room, I lifted the pillow to my face and inhaled her heavenly aroma. For a moment, I contemplated rubbing out another quick one, but I only had a half hour to change my clothes and freshen up. As I leaned over the sink to reapply my mascara and straighten my lipstick, I glanced at my Rabbit vibrator still lying on the counter. Thinking back to how the maid had nonchalantly picked it up and placed it upright next to the sink made my pussy flutter in unconscious spasms.

Fuck it, I huffed, grabbing the dildo and pulling my panties down below my knees. I've still got a few minutes, and nobody will be any the wiser if I have a little fun before heading out to another boring client dinner.

Just as I was about to thrust the oscillating tip into my sopping tunnel, I heard another soft tap on my door.

"Turndown service," a familiar voice called.

Holy shit! I gushed. *Could it be the same girl? How could I be this lucky to see her again so soon?*

"Come in," I said, thrusting my vibrator into the side pocket of the hotel robe hanging on the back of the bathroom door.

When the girl opened the door and saw me in the bathroom, I peered back at her and smiled.

"I'm just getting ready to go out," I said. "Feel free to do your thing while I finish up."

"No worries," the maid said, leaving her cart outside the door and walking toward the center of my room.

I'd always wondered what maids did during turndown service, since I'd been away from my room or too busy to be bothered when they called. But this time, I was intrigued for a number of reasons, and after composing myself in the mirror, I walked out into the room pretending to collect my things.

"I always seem to be getting in your way," I said, watching her collect the throw cushions at my headboard and neatly arranging them on the bench at the base of the bed.

"Not at all," the girl said, laying my pillows down flat on the mattress.

As she worked quietly, I peered at her gorgeous ass, perfectly framed by the white apron tied around her waist.

"I always *wondered* what you guys did during turndown service," I said, looking for an excuse to keep watching her.

She turned her head and caught me staring at her skirt.

"It's mostly just getting the bed ready for you to turn into later this evening," she smiled. "And straightening up a few things like the breakfast menu and the minibar."

I smiled, imagining she was turning *me* over instead, while she ran her hands all over my body.

"I thought it might be something a little more exotic," I mused.

"Oh?" she said. "Was there something else you wanted?"

"Um..." I hesitated for a long moment. Then I chickened out and shook my head.

"No," I said, watching her fold the sheets down into a neat triangle at the side of the bed. "You're doing everything perfectly."

"Thank you," the girl nodded, peering up at me. "I'm still kind of new to this, so any suggestions are most welcome."

"I bet you find some rooms are a little more–*unkempt*–than others," I said, reflecting back on how she'd stumbled upon my vibrator resting on the bathroom counter earlier in the day.

"Some guests are a little neater than others, to be sure," she said, taking a little extra time to plump the pillows at the head of the bed.

"But yours is easier than most," she smiled, lowering her gaze to the cleavage showing in my partially unbuttoned silk blouse.

"Do people sometimes leave things behind?" I said, hoping to steer the conversation in a new direction.

"Oh yes," she said. "Everything you can imagine. Laptops, belts, pieces of clothing–"

"And *other* personal effects?" I smiled.

"Sometimes," she blushed. "But we store everything in the lost and found in case customers want to reclaim them."

"And if they don't?" I said. "Do the housekeeping staff get to keep them as the spoils of their work?"

She placed the breakfast menu on my side table with a fresh bottle of water.

"Not usually. The hotel tries to contact them, and if we don't hear back after a certain period of time, we usually throw it out."

"That must be frustrating," I said. "I once accidentally left an expensive coat in an overhead storage bin on an airplane and never had it returned."

"They couldn't find it?" the girl enquired.

"Apparently not," I said. "I always wondered if whoever cleans the plane simply didn't report it and kept it for themselves."

"That must have been infuriating," the maid said, heading toward the bathroom to check on my supplies.

"Not so much infuriating as embarrassing," I said. "It was the *personal* effects I left in my pocket that bothered me the most."

"Yes, I can imagine," she said, returning to the side of my bed carrying my robe and a pair of terrycloth slippers. "Was it something valuable?"

"Not in monetary terms," I said, widening my eyes as she laid the robe on the edge of the mattress and placed the slippers at the side of the bed. "Just little trinkets I carry with me to keep me amused on long flights."

She felt the lump in the pocket of my robe and reached in to extract my vibrator.

"Like *this* one?" she smiled, placing it upright on the night table beside the bed. "I don't think you'll want this falling into the wrong hands."

"It depends *whose* hands it is," I smiled at her with a raised eyebrow.

The girl paused for a long moment, as we ran our eyes over one another's bodies.

"Do you mind if I ask how it works?" she asked. "I've never seen anything quite like it before."

"*Oh my God*," I said. "You haven't seen the famous Sex in the City episode where Miranda introduces her newfound sex toy to her best friends?"

"No..."

"*Come*," I said excitedly. "Scooch down next to me while I show you what this amazing device can do."

I sat down on the edge of the bed and held out my hand, pulling her down next to me. Then I grabbed the dildo off the nightstand and tapped a button on the base of the unit. I handed the shaking device to the girl, and she wrapped her hand around the shaft.

"Okay..." she said, shaking her head. "That's not so different from most vibrators."

So she has used vibrators before, I said to myself.

"That's only one of *many* ways it can stimulate you," I smiled.

I tapped another button and suddenly the chrome beads embedded inside the translucent shaft began rotating in circles.

The girl's eyes widened as she felt the beads rubbing against her palm, and she took her hand away to inspect the whirring object.

"And get *this*," I said, pressing a knob at the base of the unit.

Suddenly, the head of the penis-shaped phallus began twisting from side-to-side like a possessed wobble-head doll.

"*Holy crap*," the girl said, shifting her weight unsteadily on the bed.

"You've never had your G-spot stimulated in quite the same way until you've tried this baby," I smirked.

"Is *this* the thing you left in your coat pocket on the airplane?" she gasped.

"No, I've got a smaller and quieter device I use to keep myself amused on airplanes. Maybe I'll show you that another day. But there's one *other* feature I wanted to show you on this special toy."

I tapped another button on the base of the unit and suddenly the silicone rabbit ears extending from the side of the shaft began fluttering rapidly.

"These little fingers stimulate your clitoris while all that other action is going on inside."

"No *way*," the girl said, holding her fingers over the flapping ears.

"Do you want to give it a try?" I smiled.

"Right *here*?!" she said. "What about the other guests–"

"It won't take long, *believe* me," I said, squeezing her thigh gently. "With this multi-talented toy, you'll be satisfied in a matter of seconds."

"I don't know..." the girl hesitated, peering toward the closed door. "I don't want to get into any trouble..."

"I won't tell if you don't," I said, thrilled that she was showing newfound interest in my toy. "Here–why don't *I* show you first?"

I pulled off my clothes and threw them on the adjacent bed, then kicked off my heels and sat back against the headboard, spreading my legs.

"Oh my God..." the girl panted, peering down at my glistening labia.

Maybe this business trip isn't going to be quite so boring after all, I smiled to myself.

3

———————

"Watch and enjoy, sweetheart," I said, pointing the tip of the rotating dildo toward my opening. "*Mmm*," I moaned as it sank deeper into my tunnel.

When I'd pressed the vibrator as far as I could into my hole, I tapped the button activating the throbbing head and pulled my knees up, rocking my hips in delight. The pretty girl sat frozen on the bed, staring between my legs while I rammed the artificial cock in and out of my slurping pussy.

"You like what you see?" I said, feeling my passion rapidly rising with her watching me only inches away. "Now for the coup de grâce."

I tapped the button to activate the rabbit ears, and the flaps began buzzing against my inflamed gland. I threw my head back against the headboard and pulled the dildo harder against my snatch.

"I'm going to cum, baby," I panted, feeling the wall of pleasure about to overtake me. "Tell me your name."

"Luna," she purred, shifting closer to me on the bed.

"I'm *cumming*, Luna," I groaned as she met my gaze, yawning her mouth open in sympathy with me.

She leaned in and sucked my erect nipples into her mouth, and I whined in ecstasy from the combination of sensations that were attacking my body.

"*Fuck yes!*" I squealed, as my whole body shook like I was having an epileptic seizure. "Suck my tits baby."

I couldn't believe this heavenly angel was actually touching me while I had one of the most powerful orgasms of my life. I hadn't come so hard and so fast in a long time, but there was something incredibly hot about this sweet girl watching me while I pleasured myself.

When I finally stopped shaking, I took the dildo out of my pussy and kissed Luna on the lips. She nibbled my upper lip and I thrust my tongue into her, pulling the back of her head toward me. She moaned in my mouth, and I reached out to grasp her pointy tits, squeezing them firmly.

"Now that we've gotten to know each other a little better, my name's Jade," I smiled, unbuttoning the top of her dress. "Let's get you out of these clothes."

"Okay," she said, peering toward the door uncertainly. "But I can't take too long. My supervisor will be wondering what's holding things up..."

"I won't keep you long," I said. "Maybe we can find some more quiet time later in the evening. Don't you want to give this a try before you go?" I lifted the vibrator off the bed and flipped my legs over the side of the mattress. "Just give me a sec to wash it off first–"

"No," Luna said, pulling the Rabbit out of my hands. "I'll enjoy it more this way. It's already lubed up and ready to go."

She stood up and untied her apron, then pulled her dress down over her hips and placed it neatly on the opposite bed. Then she reached behind her back and unclasped her bra, freeing her unusually shaped tits. She had large brown areolas and thick pointy nipples, giving her boobs in the appearance of butternut squash.

Very tasty butternut squash.

"Oh my God, Luna," I said, shifting over to give her room to sit on the mattress next to me. "Come here so I can suck on those melons. You have the most delicious breasts I've ever seen."

Luna sat down next to me, and I cupped her gourds in my palms, marveling at how buoyant they were given their pointy shape.

"Do you have any idea how beautiful you are?" I said, peering into her eyes.

"My mother tells me every day," she laughed.

"I meant with other *boys and girls* your age. Surely you must notice the way they look at you."

"I guess so," she said. "I always thought it was just because I'm slightly more *curvy* than the other girls."

"You're exceptional in *so* many other ways," I said, turning her chin toward me as I kissed her gently on the lips. "Have you ever been with another lover before?"

"Just some heavy petting with the boys at school. I've never been with another woman like this before..."

I pushed the Rabbit vibrator toward the side of the bed and pinched her nipples gently between my fingers.

"Let me show you what it's like to be touched by a woman. I think you'll find you don't always need *boy* parts to be satisfied."

"But what about the Rabbit toy?" she said, peering at my glistening vibrator lying on the bed.

"There'll be plenty of time for that another time. I'm staying at the hotel for a few more days. Now lie down while I worship your body."

I pulled the corner of the sheets toward the far end of the bed, and Luna lay down flat on the mattress. Then I pulled off her panties and lay next to her while we rubbed our bodies together softly. When she felt my breasts pressing up against her, she moaned softly and I kissed her, rolling my tongue around the inside of her mouth.

"Jade," she purred. "I love the feel of your body next to me. I've wanted you to touch me from the moment I saw you working at the desk."

"Oh *really*?" I said, pulling back in surprise. "You little tease. And here I thought you were ignoring me the whole time."

"How could I ignore you after smelling your scent on the vibrator you left on the counter? And I saw the way you were looking at me—"

"Were you bending over and shaking your ass more than usual to attract my attention?"

"Maybe..." she said, nuzzling her nose into the side of my cheek.

I smiled as I sucked on her puffy lips.

"Do you know what I've been fantasizing about all day long since I saw you?" I said.

"Showing me how to use your special vibrator?" she said.

"No," I purred. "Ever since I saw you leaning over the bathroom counter, I've been dreaming about licking your sweet pussy."

"I was thinking the same thing when I saw you staring at me."

"Did it make you *wet* when you thought about my face between your legs?"

"Mmm-hmm," Luna nodded.

"Spread your legs for me, baby. Let me feel what I've been dreaming about these last few hours."

Luna fanned her legs halfway apart, and I lifted myself up to position myself in her crevasse.

"God," I grunted, kissing my way up the inside of her thighs. "You smell exquisite. What *is* that perfume you're wearing, anyway?"

"Black Opium, by Yves Saint Laurent," she said.

"How perfect," I purred, peering at her dark labia framed by the thick patch of black hair resting on top of her pubis. "Let me smell your flower."

I pulled myself closer to her opening, then breathed in her perfume through my nostrils.

"You could attract any manner of pollinator with that heavenly scent," I said. "I feel lucky to be the first one to kiss you here."

"Yes," Luna panted, lifting her pelvis off the mattress. "Lick my pussy. Taste my nectar."

Normally, I would have teased her a little longer to build up her excitement, but I didn't need any further invitation. I lowered my head and enveloped her glistening jewel in my mouth, feeling her pubic hair brushing against my forehead. She tasted as sweet as honey, and I paused for a long moment, sucking her juices into my mouth. Luna groaned and pressed her mound harder against my face, and I extended my tongue, caressing the top of her lips.

"Yes, Jade," Luca purred. "Suck my rose. Spread me open like a blossoming flower."

"Mmm," I murmured, getting increasingly turned on by the botanic metaphor. I guessed there was a lot more to this intriguing maid than just a pretty face, and I was looking forward to learning about her other interests and passions. But right now, there was only one thing on my mind. Taking her cue, I lowered my head and pressed my tongue slowly into her cavity. Luna groaned and placed her hands behind my head, pulling me harder against her vulva.

"*Fuck yes*," she grunted, gripping my hair between her fists. "Fuck my pussy with your tongue, Jade. I want to cum all over your face."

I was taken aback by her sudden raunchy turn, but her dirty language just got me more worked up as I felt my juices making a giant wet spot on the mattress between my legs. I grabbed the side of her thighs and pressed my tongue as deep into her as I could, then swirled it around in circles, tasting her syrup.

As she began to rock her hips against my face and grip my hair ever tighter, my roots started to sting, but I was so turned on by her mounting passion, I paid no attention. As she began to thrash her hips wildly against my face, I ground my own pelvis against the mattress, imagining I was fucking her with my cunny instead of my face.

Suddenly, she arched her hips off the mattress and wailed out loud as I watched her tits shaking like two melons in a hurricane. Her giant areolas stared back at me with their flaring nipples as I sucked her juices out of her twitching pussy. Luna held me tight against her vulva for many long seconds as her body twisted and convulsed against my dripping face. When she finally stopped cumming, she released her grip on my hair and flopped back against the pillows propped up against the headboard.

"Jesus, girl," I said, peering up between her legs. "You don't hold back, do you?"

"I guess I've been saving up imagining what this would feel like," she said. "Sorry if I got a little carried away. Did I hurt you?"

"Only in the best possible way," I smiled. "That might have been the sexiest thing I've ever experienced."

Luna turned her wrist to look at her watch.

"I've got to get back to work before I get into trouble. Will you have some more time for us to get back together between your business meetings?"

"Are you *kidding* me?" I said, feeling my juices dribbling down the inside of my thighs. "Screw my client. *You're* my new project for the rest of the week."

4

———

I arrived at my dinner appointment twenty minutes late, using the feeble excuse of a family emergency. But my buyer must have wondered just what kind of 'emergency' had put such severe knots in my hair and rumpled my clothing so thoroughly. But I hardly cared, reflecting back on the memory of Luna's hips quivering over my face. For the rest of the dinner, I barely heard a thing he said, as I nibbled on the red peppers in my stir-fry and swirled the red wine around my mouth, remembering her exquisite taste.

When I got back to my hotel room, I propped myself up against the bed's headboard and watched myself in the desk mirror while I fucked myself with my vibrator, imagining her looking back at me. I slept like a baby that night, then got up early to have a long shower in the morning. I wanted to be as fresh as possible when Luna returned later that morning to do my room. I kept myself busy fantasizing about all the things I wanted to do with her as I introduced her to the joys of lesbian lovemaking. But when the tap finally arrived on my door, it was a different-sounding tone that greeted me.

Hiding my vibrator under the pillow fold in the adjacent bedspread, I opened the door to see an older, frumpy-looking maid. I motioned her into my room, then collected my belongings in preparation for heading to the office. But as I watched her go about her duties, I couldn't help asking about Luna.

"What happened to the girl who cleaned my room yesterday?" I asked.

"We're assigned different rooms every day, so she's probably busy cleaning another floor. Was there something special you needed?"

"No," I said, slumping my shoulders. "I just wanted to give her an extra tip for the special housekeeping services she provided yesterday."

"You can leave it in an envelope on your pillow when you check-out of your room. I'll mention it to her, so she remembers to pick it up."

I wasn't sure if she was telling me the full truth, but I was far more concerned that I'd embarrassed Luna or somehow scared her from returning to my room. Had I come on too strong during our first encounter? Had I misread the signals that she seemed just as interested in me as I was with her? Had her manager admonished her for taking too long to finish my room?

For the rest of the day, I had a hard time concentrating on my client presentations, worrying that I'd lost my chance to reconnect with the sweet Latina beauty. I canceled my dinner plans hoping she'd return for my turndown service that evening, while flipping through the channels on my in-room TV to keep myself distracted. When I heard a soft tap on my door, I practically leapt off my bed, feeling my heart racing in excitement. I tiptoed to the door and peered through the peephole. I was delighted to see Luna standing there with another pretty girl about her same age, both dressed in casual clothes.

I swung open the door and peered at her inquisitively.

"I wasn't sure if I was going to see you again," I said, pinching my eyebrows in dismay.

"Sorry," Luna said, turning her head both ways to glance down the empty hallway. "It was my day off today, and I didn't want any of the other hotel staff seeing me entering your room. We're not supposed to mingle with the guests."

"Of course," I said, looking at her pretty companion. "Did you have any special plans? Would you like to go out for some drinks?"

"This is my friend Gabriella," Luna said. "She works with me at the hotel. Do you mind if I bring her along?"

"Of course not," I said, smiling at the other girl. "I just need a moment to freshen up before heading out. Would you like to come in while I get ready?"

"Sure," Luna said.

I stuck my head out the door to make sure it was clear, then I ushered the two girls into my room.

"I was afraid I might have scared you away after we met yesterday. The new maid wasn't entirely sure where you were."

"I'm sorry..." Luna hesitated. "I didn't have your number and I–"

I noticed the girls shifting their weight awkwardly in the narrow walkway next to my bathroom and I motioned them toward the side of my bed.

"Would you like to make yourselves comfortable while I straighten myself up?"

"Yes, thank you."

I went into the washroom to put on some lipstick and leaned over the sink, trying to see their reflection in the mirror. I had no idea why she'd decided to bring a friend, but my pussy twitched wondering if they might be lovers.

"I didn't catch your friend's name," I called from the bathroom.

"Gabriella," Luna said. "We started around the same time."

"At the hotel? What do you do, Gabriella?"

"I'm a waitress in the downstairs restaurant," she replied.

"You're both so pretty," I said. "I can only imagine how many times you get propositioned by lonely middle-aged travelers."

"It's not so bad," Gabriella said. "As long as we keep a healthy distance and don't flirt too much, we manage to stay out of trouble."

I smiled, remembering how easy it was to lure Luna into my bed.

"Have you known each other very long?" I said, fishing for more details about their personal relationship.

"Just a few months," Luna said. "We kind of hit it off right away."

I was intrigued why Luna would bring her friend to our second date, knowing how sexually charged it was likely to be. As I stepped out of the lavatory brushing my hair, I caught them inspecting my Rabbit vibrator as they giggled quietly between them. I guessed that they'd seen it sticking out from under the covers, and Luna must have been describing its various features. When she tried to stuff it back under the pillow, I held up my hand.

"Don't put it away on *my* account," I smiled. "Have you ever seen one of those before, Gabriella?"

"I Googled it after Luna told me about it," she said. "I've just seen what it looks like on their website."

"It's hard to appreciate it from a *picture*," I said, pulling it back out from under the covers and sitting down on the bed next to Gabriella. "Here, why don't you press some of the buttons and see for yourself."

I handed the purple dildo to her, and she fumbled with it awkwardly.

"Press the little button on the left-hand side of the controller," I said.

Gabriella tapped it, and the chrome beads began whirring in circles around the middle of the shaft. She jumped in surprise and looked up at me inquisitively.

"I bet you've never seen a boy's cock do *that* before," I smiled.

"Um, no..." she said, blushing softly.

"Try *this* one," I said, pointing to the button just below it.

When she tapped it, the penis-shaped head of the dildo began twisting like a spinning top and she almost dropped it in her lap.

"I *know*," I nodded. "If only *every* man could be equipped that way."

"What are these strange things on the side?" she said, pointing to the flexible rabbit ears.

"That's what *really* makes this special," I grinned, suspecting that Luna had already described the unique features of my vibrator in meticulous detail. I tapped the button on the bottom of the device, and the rabbit ears began flapping rapidly. "These two little fingers stimulate your clitoris while the rest of the vibrator is turning around inside you."

I peered up at Gabriella, then smiled at Luna.

"But you already *knew* that, didn't you? I'm sure Luna's already given you a full accounting of its various functions. You didn't just come here for a few *drinks*, did you?"

"Um..." Luna hesitated, peering over at her friend.

"It's okay," I said, taking the vibrator out of her hands and placing it on the nightstand next to my bed. "I'm glad you brought a friend. There's *so* many more ways we can enjoy this together."

I stood up and took off my clothes, throwing the pieces on the bed next to them, then pulled down the covers on the adjacent bed.

"You never know when double beds might come in handy on a business trip," I grinned.

While I stood in front of the two girls completely naked, they ran their eyes over my figure, lingering especially long at my glistening, hairless mound. Then I held out my hand to Gabriella and motioned for her to join me on the opposite bed.

"Come," I said. "Something tells me this isn't the first time you girls have experimented with sex toys. Let me show you how the *three* of us can make this a little more fun."

I lifted Gabriella off the bed, then pulled her turtleneck over her head and slowly unclasped her bra. Her breasts were smaller than Luna's, but rounder and firmer, with pink areolas and small button-shaped nipples. I cupped them gently, then leaned in to give her a wet kiss.

"You're beautiful, Gabriella," I gushed. "I can see why the two of you came together so quickly. I haven't seen such a pretty pair in a long time."

I peered down at her tight jeans, admiring the youthful contour of her hips.

"Do you need help getting out of those pants?"

"Yes please," she said as I watched her nipples contract and harden in excitement.

I reached down and unclasped the button at the top of her waistband, then lowered the zipper and pulled her jeans down to the floor as she kicked them off to the side. Then I kneeled down between her thighs and pulled her panties down to the floor, and she stepped out of them. Her bush was trimmed more neatly than Luna's, with a tawny amber color, and I leaned in to kiss it while I reached around and cupped her buttocks gently. Her ass quivered as I lowered my mouth to her moist slit, and she gasped when I circled her nub with my lips.

"Mmm," I moaned, as she pressed her mound harder into my face.

I peered out of the side of my eyes at Luna still sitting on the edge of the other bed, noticing her hand moving gently in her lap. The thought of her watching me while I ate out her best friend thrilled me, and I began to roll my hips unconsciously as I licked and teased Gabriella's burning clit.

"Uhnn," she grunted, spreading her legs further apart and angling her hips until she was standing directly over top of me. I squeezed her cheeks while her buttocks clenched together, and from the pace of her breathing I knew it wouldn't be long before she reached the peak of her pleasure.

I tilted my head up and watched her little boobs bouncing on her chest as she ran her fingers through my hair. She wasn't as aggressive as Luna had been holding me while I sucked her pussy, and I guessed that she was the submissive one in the relationship.

"Oh *God*," Gabriella suddenly moaned as she slumped over me, jerking her body in spastic movements.

I could tell from the intensity of her rocking motion that she was cumming on my face, and I held her tightly until she stopped moving. I pulled my head back and peered over at Luna, who had her knees spread wide apart and was rubbing her hand vigorously over a large stain in the crotch of her jeans.

"I think somebody *else* is missing out on all the fun," I said, shifting over and pulling her pants down over her curvy hips.

This time she'd chosen to go pantyless, and I looked up at her with a mischievous smile.

"Were you in a hurry to get started tonight?" I grinned.

"Going bare just reminded me of what it felt like to have you next to me," she smiled. "I didn't want anything else getting in the way."

I pulled her off the bed and ripped off her T-shirt, thrilled to see her oval-shaped melons bouncing freely on her chest.

"*Gawd*, how I've fantasized about these since I last saw you," I panted, pulling her toward me, mashing our bodies together. "But first, I had something different in mind."

I yanked the opposite bedspread all the way down toward the baseboard and instructed the two girls to kneel on the mattress, facing one another.

"I want to watch you enjoy my special vibrator together."

I handed the dildo to Gabriella and smiled.

"Why don't you place the long end inside, then press your bodies together so you can *both* enjoy the vibrating rabbit ears?"

Gabriella looked at Luna, and her friend nodded back at her.

"Knock yourselves out while I make myself more comfortable," I smiled.

I leaned back on my mattress and began circling my clit while I watched the two girls rubbing their bodies together. Gabriella tapped the buttons on the base of the unit and slowly inserted the oscillating device into her hole. She gasped in surprise at the unusual sensation, and Luna wrapped her arms around her shoulders, pulling their bodies together. As Gabriella began to thrust the humming vibrator in and out of her pussy, Luna pressed her mound against her girl-friend, purring in delight.

"Press the knob on the bottom now," I said to Gabriella, inserting two fingers into my slit.

Gabriella peered over at me, and her eyes widened as she watched me finger-fucking myself with my knees spread wide apart. She reached behind her ass and flexed her finger, and I heard a loud buzzing sound emanating from between their legs. The two girls groaned in pleasure as they felt the rabbit ears flapping against their joined clits, then they pressed their faces together, tonguing each other wildly. The image of the two sexy girls rubbing their bodies together as the big dildo whirled, twisted, and buzzed between both of their legs was surreal.

"*Fuck* yes," I hissed, ramming my fingers harder into my cunt. "Rub your tits and cunnies together while I watch you come."

"Mmm," Luna moaned, placing her hands over Gabriella's buttocks. "Come with me, Gabby," she said. "I can feel the rabbit ears touching both of our clits."

"Yes," Gabby whinnied, reaching around to grab Luna's ass at the same time. "I'm cumming, Lou. Oh *God*, I'm *cumming!*"

The two girls tilted their heads back and wailed in unison as their bodies began to quiver and tremble in simultaneous orgasm. I'd been so focused on watching them rubbing their bodies together that I'd barely paid any attention to what *I* was feeling, but the sight of them cumming together with my favorite vibrator purring between their legs quickly put me over the edge. I lifted my hips off the bed and thrust my fingers deep into my snatch and uttered a deep, guttural moan.

"Fuck *me*," I said, feeling my pussy clamp down hard over my fingers as my body levitated a foot above of the mattress. I held my body in this arched position for many long seconds while the three of us grunted and screamed in simultaneous ecstasy.

Suddenly I remembered where we were, and how thin the walls were between the adjoining rooms.

I wonder if all the other guests are expecting a similar type of turndown service, I smiled, flopping down onto the mattress in exhaustion.

5

——————

When the girls lay down on the bed after coming down from their tandem orgasm, I nestled in next to them, and we cuddled silently for a few minutes. It felt incredible to have two gorgeous angels lying next to me as we nibbled and caressed each other's bodies, with nobody wanting to acknowledge what had just happened. But as they became progressively more daring in exploring my body, Luna pulled away and peered at her friend.

"I think it's *Jade's* turn now to get a little direct attention, don't you think Gabby?"

Gabriella nodded, and Luna turned her head toward me, lifting the Rabbit vibrator off the bed.

"How can we put this thing to work for all *three* of us?" she said. "We have too many body parts for one device to stimulate us at the same time."

I raised myself up on one arm and pushed the vibrator back down onto the mattress.

"I think each of us have had plenty enough stimulation from that thing. I'd far rather play with some flesh and blood pretty *girls* than have another cock inside me."

"Mmm," Luna grinned. "What can we do for *you* now that you've given us so much pleasure?"

I peered at Luna's tubular breasts and smiled.

"I've been fantasizing all day about you fucking me with those pretty melons. I want you to diddle me with your special tits."

"Okay," she said, lifting an eyebrow. "But what about Gabby? It seems such a waste for her to just stand by and *watch*."

I peered over at Gabriella and hesitated as I contemplated how to get all three of us involved at the same time. Then a huge grin slowly spread over my face.

"I have an idea," I said. "I'll lie down on the bed while Gabby straddles my face, as you lift up my hips and support me from behind. That way, you both can get a bird's-eye view of the action while I get serviced from both sides."

Luna's eyes opened wide as saucers as she pictured the scene in her mind.

"Holy shit," she said. "That will be so hot. Plus, we can *both* play with your pretty pussy from that position!"

"What are you waiting for?" I said, lying down with my ass pointed toward the headboard. "Come here little girl and sit on my face."

Gabriella got up on her hands and knees and placed her legs on opposite sides of my head facing Luna. As she slowly lowered her dripping pussy onto my face, Luna raised my hips off the bed and pressed her chest into my lower back until my body was perpendicular to the mattress. Then she spread her knees for support and pushed my legs apart. As my feet dangled in the air beside her shoulders, she grabbed one of her tits and pointed her erect teat toward my quivering hole. When I felt her flesh press against my vulva, I grunted into Gabriella's pussy writhing over my face.

"*Uhhn*," I groaned, unable to speak with my mind spinning in pleasure.

When Luna began rubbing her breast up and down my slit, I could hear the soft sloshing sound my pussy made as my labia puckered in and out in involuntary reflex. Although I couldn't see what she was doing with Gabby's ass buried over my face, the thought of them both looking at my upturned pussy drove me wild with pleasure.

Just when I thought it couldn't get any better, Gabby leaned forward and encircled my inflamed bud with her lips, rolling her tongue over my gland while she squeezed my tits. With her head now getting in the way of Luna's titfucking, her friend lowered her face down my perineum and began licking my freshly washed pucker.

I couldn't believe that every part of my body was now being serviced by these two angels, and I grunted in mounting ecstasy as my hips began to shake from my approaching orgasm. When it finally hit me, I growled like a wild animal while Gabriella pressed her pussy hard against my face and moaned along with me as she sucked my inflamed bean like a lollypop. When I felt Luna's tits rubbing against the back of my hips, my juices spurted out of me like a geyser, spraying all over both of the girls' faces.

I came for the longest time as the two girls held my body in this upright position, quivering and spurting while the entire length of my perineum flexed in powerful contractions. I wondered if Luna noticed my rosebud clenching in powerful contractions from her front-row seat immediately above my elevated pelvis. Either way, the thought of my most intimate parts exposed to their direct view as I came mere inches away from both of their faces magnified my arousal as I grunted under the weight of Gabby's trembling hips. When I finally stopped cumming, Luna lowered my hips back down onto the mattress and both girls lay beside me, caressing my drenched tits and abdomen.

"Oh my God," I panted, watching stars floating above my head as my mind spun in a drunken stupor. "That was even hotter than I imagined. I don't think I've come that hard in my entire life."

"We *noticed*," Luna smiled, wiping my juices off her face with the back of her hand. "You really opened the taps unexpectedly on the two of us."

"Sorry. I do that when I'm especially turned on. And I've never been stimulated like that before. That was incredible."

"We enjoyed it just as much as you did," Gabriella said, sucking my nipples softly into her mouth.

"Really?" I said, holding her head gently against my chest. "I couldn't tell with your hips buried on top of my face. Did you cum too? I didn't want to leave you hanging–"

"Oh, I *came* alright. Maybe not with the same degree of fireworks that you did, but when you started squirting all over my face, you opened the taps for me too. I've never been in a threesome before. Thanks for inviting me into your room."

I peered over at Luna and smiled.

"I think we have your friend to thank for that. I'm guessing this isn't the first time the two of you have had girl-on-girl sex before."

"No," Gabriella blushed. "But never quite like this."

6

"You know," I said, smiling at the two girls, realizing I had a once-in-a-lifetime opportunity. "We don't have a lot of time left before I have to leave town. We should make the best of our remaining time together."

"What else did you have in mind?" Luna said, propping herself up on an elbow.

"Everything we've done so far has been one-on-one, or just two girls enjoying each other's bodies. We still haven't had a chance for all *three* of us to come together yet."

Luna peered up at me and smiled.

"I have to confess that I was touching myself while I rubbed my breasts against your pussy," she said. "I came soon after I saw both of you climaxing."

"That makes me happy," I said, leaning in to kiss her moist lips. "But I was thinking of something even *more* interactive. Something where we all can be joined together at the same time."

The girls peered at me with a confused expression, shaking their heads.

"How is that even *possible*?" Gabriella said, pinching her eyebrows.

"With each of us having separate lady parts, how would we be able to touch them together simultaneously?"

"Surely you two have experimented with different types of *scissoring*?" I smiled.

"Yes..." Gabby blushed.

"Have you ever tried it *back-to-back*?" I said.

"How do you mean?" Luna said.

"I mean *ass-to-ass*. Two of us could rub our vulvas together, with the third one lying underneath as we ground our mounds together. I've never actually tried it, but I'm thinking it might work if we position ourselves the right way."

"I'm up for giving it a try," Luna smiled. "But who'll be on top and who'll be on the bottom?"

I looked at Luna and grinned.

"Something tells me you like to be the dominant one," I said. "Besides, I still haven't had quite enough of you. I've been dreaming about cunt-fucking you ever since I laid eyes on you. What do you say, Gabby? Would you like to have two sexy girls rubbing their pussies over top of you while you wrap your legs around our asses?"

"Oh my God," she gushed, turning her head toward Luna. "You weren't kidding when you told me about this crazy woman. I'm almost cumming just *thinking* about it!"

"It's *your* turn to lie down on the bed, girl," I instructed. "Would you like to take the inferior or superior position, Luna?"

Luna paused for a moment as she looked at me, trying to interpret my meaning. Then she nodded her head and smiled.

"I'll face her lower body, while you play with Gabby's tits. That way, I can watch her pussy twitching when we all come together."

"Works for me," I smiled, lifting my knee and placing my legs on opposite sides of Gabriella's hips.

Luna turned around and did the same thing, but with her head pointed toward Gabby's feet. We shifted our weight slightly backwards and when our asses touched, we arched our backs, angling our vulvas toward one another. When we felt our clits touch, each of us groaned.

"*Fuck*, yes," Luna hissed. "I want to feel you spray all over my ass when you come this time, Jade."

"My pleasure, hun," I said, peering into Gabby's eyes. "What do you say, Gab, are you ready to give this a try?"

"Damn *straight*," she said, pulling my head down and thrusting her tongue deep into my mouth.

As I swiveled my hips against Luna's ass and dripping pussy, I mashed my tits against Gabriella's chest, listening to her groan in my mouth. She tilted her hips and lifted her buttocks off the bed as I felt her grinding her mound against mine.

"That's it, baby," I purred. "Fuck my pussy while Luna tribs my ass. I'm going to spray all over your pretty cunny when I come."

"Mmm," Gabby moaned as I kissed her wildly.

The three of us were twisting our hips and grinding our pussies together, trying to find the right position where each of our clits received the ideal stimulation. I could feel Luna's labia intermingling with my own, and our pussies made nasty slurping noises as our asses smacked together. While our mutual passion escalated into a noisy cacophony of grunts and moans, Gabriella wrapped her arms and legs around my back and pressed her chest harder against my tits as she began to make funny squealing noises.

I knew she was close to cumming and as my *own* pleasure began to crest, I could feel it rushing toward me like a freight train. When the orgasm suddenly washed over me, the walls of my pussy suddenly clamped down hard and I began gushing all over Luna's bare ass and Gabby's pussy. Luna's buttocks began quaking next to mine as she howled in delight watching her girlfriend's vulva slapping open and shut in the throes of her own powerful climax. All three of us were climaxing now as we ground our pussies together in glorious union, grasping and clutching each other wildly. As we quivered, dripped, and squirted in mutual ecstasy for what seemed like an eternity, I suddenly became aware of how soaked the sheets had become.

It's going to be one hell of a clean-up operation for the next housekeeper,

I smiled. *But no matter—with the generous tip I plan to leave on my pillow when I check out, something tells me she won't mind.*

THE EXCHANGE STUDENT

AN EROTIC ADVENTURE

1

I almost missed the ad while rushing out of the grocery store after a long day of work. Tucked away in a corner of the bulletin board near the exit door was a small poster with the headline *Earn Extra Income Hosting a Foreign Exchange Student*. I paused for a moment, then pulled my cart closer to the board to read the message:

Earn money while helping a foreign student expand their cultural horizons. There's no better way to learn a new language and appreciate other cultures than to live with someone from another part of the world. By hosting a young person from a different country, you promote friendship, understanding, and cooperation in your home and community. Welcome a foreign exchange student into your home today and open the door to an exciting new world of experiences. Contact exchangehost.com for more info.

After reading the ad, I suddenly became aware of how hard my heart was pounding in my chest. I'd lived alone after separating from my husband more than two years ago, and my big house had become far too quiet and lonely. Having never had children of my own, the idea of hosting a young person from another country seemed a perfect fit. I'd have someone to liven up my daily routine while helping the student develop a sense of independence in an exciting new environment.

When I got home, I went to the agency's website and read everything I could about the program. The more I learned, the more excited I became. I wasn't interested in the small monthly stipend I'd earn hosting the student so much as the sense of adventure taking in a boarder from a different country. It would be an opportunity to share cultural experiences, improve my foreign language skills, and make new friendships.

The following morning, I called first thing to book an appointment for an interview. When I got to their office, the receptionist escorted me into the director's suite where a smartly dressed woman in her fifties invited me to make myself comfortable while she took a seat in the opposite armchair.

"Welcome, Ms. Robertson," she said. "My name is Elise Laurent, the director of Exchange Host student exchange services. What brings you to our office today?"

"I'm interested in hosting a foreign exchange student," I said.

"I see you're here by yourself. Do you live alone?"

"Yes," I said, crossing my legs defensively. "Do you accept applications from single women?"

"Of course," she said. "It all depends on the individual's circumstances and motivation. Our primary concern is finding a safe and supportive environment for our clients. May I ask what attracts you to our program?"

"I saw an ad for your services at the supermarket. I've never had any children, and I like the idea of helping a young person supplement their education in a different country. With so much conflict and misunderstanding between countries and cultures, this seems an ideal way to foster better communication and friendship."

"You seem primarily focused on the benefits to the *student*," the director nodded. "What advantages do you see for you, personally?"

"It's not about the money, if that's what you mean. I'd do it for free, if that were an option. I live alone and work from home, so I have limited opportunity for social interaction. To be honest, I think it would be fun to have someone else to share my house with. Especially a young person who I could foster and take under my wing. I could take her shopping, go out to restaurants, visit national parks–it could be fun for both of us."

"So you're looking to host a female student only?"

"Not necessarily. I'd consider either gender, but I think it would be more fun hosting a girl."

The director nodded, scribbling some notes on a notepad.

"You say money isn't a consideration. May I ask what you do for a living?"

"I'm a freelance graphic artist. I help develop ads, logos, websites, and media campaigns for corporate clients."

"Do you own your home?"

"I guess technically the bank owns it until the mortgage is paid off," I chuckled. "But yes, I'm the sole title owner."

"Umm," the director hummed, scribbling some more notes. "Do you have an extra room and bath available for another occupant?"

"Yes," I said. "Frankly, that's another reason I'm considering this. My house is far too large for one person. I'll feel better making better use of the extra space and helping the environment by wasting less."

"Um-hmm," the Ms. Laurent nodded. "And you feel you'll have enough free time away from your work and other responsibilities to give your charge proper attention and care? It's not like taking in a boarder–these students will need oversight and companionship. They'll be a long way from home in a whole new environment. It's more akin to a foster parent situation."

"Absolutely," I said. "Being self-employed means I can make my own hours and work around my guest's schedule. I'm looking forward to taking her under my wing and making a new friend. Like I said, I'm not doing it for the money."

"Okay," the woman said, putting down her notepad. "We'll need you to fill in an application and provide three references. Then I'll need your approval to run a criminal record check and credit check. If everything pans out, we'll begin contacting you with possible candidates to find a good fit. The whole process can take two or three months and with a new school year approaching, you'll need to get started soon."

"Sounds good," I said, rising from my chair and extending my hand. "Thank you for your time and assistance, Ms. Laurent. I'll look forward to hearing back from you at your earliest opportunity. Let me know if you need any more information in the meantime."

"It's been my pleasure," she said. "Thank you for your interest in our program. I think you'll find this experience enriching and rewarding on both sides. My assistant will help you with the paper-work. We'll be in touch soon."

After filling in the application, I drove home with a sense of excitement wondering who the agency would find to connect me with. I had no idea what age, sex, or nationality the student would be and that was part of the attraction. It would be a whole new experience for both of us. But after a few weeks of not hearing from the agency, I began to wonder if they were having second thoughts about my candidacy. I'd checked with my references who told me they'd already been contacted, and I knew there wouldn't be any issues with my background or credit check, so with only a few weeks left before the start of the new school year, I placed a call to the director.

"Exchange Host," the receptionist said, answering the phone.

"May I speak with Ms. Laurent?" I said.

"May I ask who's calling?"

"My name is Jade Robertson. I had an interview with Ms. Laurent a couple of months ago and haven't heard back. I was just hoping for an update."

"One moment please," the receptionist said.

"Hello, Ms. Robertson," the director said when she picked up her extension.

"I'm sorry to bother you," I said. "But I haven't heard back from you and I know we're getting close to the start of another academic year. I was wondering if you had any problems with my application or if you'd vetted any potential candidates."

"No," the director said. "Your application came through with flying colors. Unfortunately, it was processed a bit late and all of the hosting spots for the new school year have been filled."

"That's disappointing to hear," I said. "So I guess I'll have to wait another year for consideration?"

"Not necessarily," she said. "We have a number of students who seek to transfer mid-year. There may be another opportunity as we approach the end of the first semester. We'll contact you if anything becomes available."

"Okay, thank you, Ms. Laurent."

I hung up, feeling dejected about prematurely getting my hopes up. The closer we'd gotten to the start of the school year, the more excited I'd become about having a new housemate. Now I'd have to wait a whole other year to have the opportunity to host a student.

For a while, I considered putting an ad in the local university newspaper offering a room for board, but I knew it wouldn't be the same. There was something about taking in a young international student that added an extra allure for me. I'd have the chance to nurture someone who really depended on me while we explored each other's language and culture. In the end, I decided to hold off, hoping to try again next year.

But much to my surprise, I received a message from Ms. Laurent a couple of months later indicating that she had a new candidate lined up for the spring semester. I picked up the phone and called her immediately.

"Hello, Ms. Laurent," I said excitedly when she picked up the phone. "It's Jade Robertson. I got your message regarding a possible candidate for the spring semester, and I'm still interested."

"That's wonderful news," she said. "We're ready to finalize the placement if you're sure you're ready to proceed."

"Absolutely," I said, still catching my breath.

"Would you like to view the student's profile before making a final commitment? We can send it to you via email if you prefer."

I paused for a moment, hearing my heart pounding in my chest. As eager as I was for more details, I couldn't wait for the most important information.

"That would be helpful, thank you," I said. "Can you tell me if it's a boy or a girl, and from which country they'll be transferring?"

"It's a girl who'll be completing the final semester for her senior year. She's transferring in from France."

France, I thought, feeling my heart skip a beat. I'd always wanted to travel there and learn to speak the language, but had never found the time. This would be my chance to learn more about their culture by experiencing it in a whole *different* way.

"That sounds exciting," I said. "When will she be arriving, and are there any final preparation requirements?"

"She's due to arrive January twenty-third, the weekend between first and second semester. The only other preparation requirement is a final in-home interview to ensure you have sufficient accommodation and resources to care for your guest. We can arrange a convenient time to visit next week if that will work for you."

"That's perfect. How about Wednesday at one p.m.? Thank you for keeping me in the queue for consideration with this placement."

"My pleasure, Ms. Robertson. I'll look forward to seeing you next Wednesday. Bye for now."

Later that day, I received the student profile via email. When I opened it, the first thing I saw was a single headshot photo. It was a bit grainy, but she looked pretty and fresh-faced, with wavy blonde hair and bright blue-green eyes. Her name was Luna, and she lived in Saint Denis, a suburb of Paris. She listed her hobbies as yoga, skiing, and dressmaking. Her father was an engineer and her mother was a nurse. She had two siblings, an older sister and a younger brother. Her career interests were international relations and fashion design.

Perfect, I thought. *We can exercise together, go skiing on weekends, and we both have an interest in women's fashion.* It sounded like a match made in heaven.

After successfully passing the home inspection and knowing I'd have a girl as my guest, I went about decorating her room like I was expecting a newborn baby. I went out and bought a new work desk and bookshelf at Ikea and new towels and linens from Bed, Bath, and Beyond. The closer I got to her arrival date, the more excited I became about having my new houseguest. For the next four or five months, I knew my life would never be the same.

2

As Luna's arrival date approached, I busied myself tidying up her room, decorating it with girly stuff. I painted the walls pale blue, bought lots of pretty throw pillows, and hung a beautiful photo of the Eiffel Tower to remind her of home. I even picked up a basket of beauty products from the French store L'Occitane, including lavender-scented bubble bath, shea-butter soap, and cherry blossom shampoo and conditioner. I wanted to do everything I could to make her adjustment as smooth as possible.

When her arrival date finally came, I drove with Ms. Laurent from the placement agency to O'Hare airport. While we waited outside the International Arrivals lounge, I tapped my foot nervously, checking my watch every two minutes wondering what was holding her up.

"Shouldn't she be here by now?" I said to Ms. Laurent. "Her flight arrived more than an hour ago."

"This is normal for international arrivals," she said, holding a sign with Luna's name on it as passengers began steaming out of the terminal. "She still has to clear through immigration, pick up her checked bags at the baggage carousel, and find her way through this maze of an airport."

"Does she have your phone number in case she gets lost?"

"Yes, but I'm sure it won't come to that," she said, placing her hand on my forearm, trying to calm me down. "Don't worry, there's only one exit from her arrival terminal, and she was told that we'd be waiting with a sign."

I scanned the swarm of passengers exiting the baggage claim area, trying to recognize her face from the picture in her profile. After another fifteen minutes or so, I saw a young girl throw up her hand and move toward us. When she reached our position, she stood her roller bags on the floor and reached out her hand to Ms. Laurent.

"Madame Laurent?" she said with a lilting French accent.

"Bonjour, Luna," Ms. Laurent said with an equally strong accent. "Comment était votre vol?"

"C'était bien," the girl said, shaking her head in dismay. "Mais c'est un très grand aéroport!"

"Je suis désolé," Ms. Laurent replied. "Je suis content que tu ne t'es pas perdu."

Then the director turned to face me, extending her hand in my direction.

"May I introduce you to your American host, Ms. Jade Robertson?"

"Pleased to meet you, Ms. Robertson," the girl said in perfect English.

"Please, call me Jade," I said, shaking her hand softly as she bent her knees in a gentle curtsy.

I was immediately taken by how beautiful she was up close and in person. She had wavy blond hair with a tinge of red, falling softly over her emerald-green eyes and creamy skin. With her high cheekbones, gently upturned nose and plump, rosebud lips, she looked like a young fashion model straight out of Vogue magazine. Wearing a sheepskin-lined leather bomber jacket overtop skinny jeans and Converse sneakers, I could see how she'd already defined her own unique sense of style.

"Do you need to use the restroom or get something to eat?" Ms. Laurent asked the girl.

"I had a snack on the plane, thank you," she said. "And I found the *toilette* in the baggage claim area."

Even the way she pronounced everyday pedestrian words like toilet in her native tongue was charming. I was already swooning over her, and I'd only met her for a few minutes.

"Can we help you with your bags?" Ms. Laurent said.

"Yes, thank you," the girl said. "I'm really getting a workout juggling these three bags."

Ms. Laurent reached out for the large check bag and I grabbed the smaller carry-on roller while Luna hiked her large tote bag over her shoulder.

"Let's get you situated, then," Ms. Laurent said, pulling the large roller bag in the direction of the ground transportation exit door. "Our car isn't parked too far away."

We packed Luna's bags in the trunk of my car, and I invited her to sit in the front passenger seat while Ms. Laurent sat in the back. As we exited the parking garage and pulled onto the 294 ring road heading south, Luna peered out the side window at the passing cityscape of downtown Chicago.

"You live in a very tall city," she said, gazing at the skyscrapers with wide eyes.

"Yes, I suppose it is," I nodded. "But Paris is a large city too. Doesn't it have a lot of skyscrapers also?"

"Very few, and they're all outside the main city. The city planners banned tall buildings to preserve its unique European flavor. Except for the Eiffel Tower, of course."

"Paris sounds so beautiful," I nodded. "I really must go there soon."

"Perhaps I can return the favor and host you when you visit?" Luna said, peering over at me through long eyelashes.

"That would be lovely," I said, almost missing my exit heading west toward the Naperville suburbs.

"So you live outside the city also?" Luna asked.

"Yes, but I'm only about twenty miles or so from downtown."

"I'm not familiar with miles..."

"That's equivalent to about thirty kilometers," Ms. Laurent chimed in from the back seat.

"Sorry," I said, reaching over to clasp Luna's hand gently. "I'll have to get in the habit of speaking European."

"Not at all," she said. "I'm a guest in your country. It's better that I begin learning about your American culture right away."

When we pulled into my driveway, I removed Luna's bags from the trunk and she peered up at my two-story house.

"What a beautiful home you have, Ms. Roberts–I mean, Jade," she said. "Everything in America is so *big*!"

"Thank you," I smiled. "But this really is just a typical middle-class home here in Chicago. Hopefully, you'll find plenty of room to stretch out. Come, let me show you around."

I escorted Luna and Ms. Laurent through the front door into the foyer, then hung their coats in the closet. Luna was wearing a tight cashmere sweater that matched the color of her eyes, and it took every ounce of my willpower to keep my gaze focused above her prominent, pointy breasts sitting high on her chest. We walked down the hall toward the kitchen, and I placed her bags at the foot of the stairs to the second floor. When she noticed the covered pool in my backyard, she rushed toward the window excitedly.

"You have a *pool* also?" she said. "Ms. Laurent never mentioned that!"

"Unfortunately, it's not much use during the long winter months," I said. "Hopefully we can get it up and running before you head back home." Then I pointed to the hot tub resting in the corner by the exit door. "But I *do* have a Jacuzzi that's quite relaxing on a cold winter day."

"I feel like I'm staying at a luxury hotel," Luna said.

"I wouldn't go that far," I smiled. "But I'm glad you find the accommodations suitable so far."

Ms. Laurent placed her briefcase atop the kitchen island and flipped it open.

"Shall we go over the final arrangements?" she said. "I think it's time you two settled in and begin getting to know one another."

"Certainly," I said. "Why don't you make yourselves comfortable in the living room? Can I get either of you a cup of coffee or tea?"

"Tea will be fine, thank you," Ms. Laurent said.

"Milk and sugar?"

"A little bit of both, thank you."

"Luna?"

"I'll have mine plain, thank you."

Plain it is, I thought, beginning to make a mental note of her preferences. But everything about this girl screamed she was anything but plain.

After I prepared the tea, I brought the cups into the living room and sat down on the sofa next to Luna.

"I've already gone over the protocol with both of you at some length," Ms. Laurent said. "So I won't bore you with too many more details. I just wanted to reiterate to Luna that as your official stateside sponsor, if you have any questions or concerns at any time, feel free to reach out to me at the number I've provided. That applies equally to you, Ms. Robertson. If you have any questions about legal matters or if any issues arise, please don't hesitate to give me a call."

"I've gone over the care package many times," I said, smiling at Luna as she beamed at me with a slight flush in her cheeks. "Everything looks pretty straightforward. I'm sure Luna and I will get along famously."

Ms. Laurent had us sign the final releases, then she glanced at her phone as it buzzed softly on the coffee table.

"It looks like my taxi is here," she said. "I'll look forward to hearing how you're enjoying your new surroundings, Luna. We'll talk again soon."

After I escorted Ms. Laurent to the front door and watched her pull out of the driveway, I helped Luna carry her bags upstairs to the guest bedroom.

"This is your room," I said, placing her bags by the bed. "I've tried to decorate it with a light feminine touch and some accents from your home country."

Luna peered around the room and smiled when she saw the framed print of the Eiffel Tower.

"It's lovely," she said. "You needn't have gone to so much trouble."

"It's the least I could do for someone visiting America for the first time. Let me show you your bath."

I led her into the washroom across the hall from her room, opening the empty storage lockers.

"Although it isn't attached to your room directly, you'll have the exclusive use of this bathroom. I've cleared out all the cabinets and bought you some toiletries to get you started."

Luna picked up the scented soap in the basket and held it softly under her nose.

"You've gone to so much trouble for me already, Jade," she said, peering up at me through her thick locks of hair. "It's *already* beginning to feel like home."

"I'm glad," I smiled. "Why don't you unpack, then if you'd like, we can go to the supermarket together and get some food for dinner. Or would you prefer to go out to a restaurant?"

"There's no need to treat me any different than any other houseguest," she said. "How does that American expression go? I don't want to eat you out of house and home."

As I watched her bend over to peer inside the shower curtains, I couldn't help staring at her tight, heart-shaped ass.

God forgive me, I said to myself. *Remember, you're her guardian while she's away from home. Get your mind out of the gutter.*

There was something about this precocious French beauty that told me she was going to be much more than just an ordinary houseguest.

3

———————

After Luna finished unpacking, we went to the supermarket together and picked up some food for dinner. I wanted to spoil her on her first day in the U.S., so I baked a prime rib roast with mashed potatoes and gravy, corn on the cob, and apple pie. We chatted about her interests and life experiences, and when I learned that she'd recently turned eighteen, I couldn't help seeing her in a whole new light. She seemed more mature than other girls her age, talking about how the move to a new country to finish out her last year of high school was driven by her desire for independence and to explore new opportunities.

The following day, we went shopping for school supplies, and I got her a new SIM card for her mobile phone so she could make local calls. It was a colder January than usual in Chicago, and when we got home, I invited her to join me in the hot tub. She hadn't packed a swimsuit, and knowing it was too early to invite her to go nude, I offered her my one-piece suit. We were roughly the same dress size, but her waist was definitely narrower and her breasts were firmer and pointier than mine. Before we lowered ourselves into the bubbling water, I admired her tight figure, feeling my pussy throb as the hot liquid enveloped my hips.

"Wow," Luna said, feeling the Jacuzzi jets swirling over her body under the churning water. "You weren't kidding about how relaxing this is. This feels heavenly."

"It's especially nice on a cold winter day," I nodded. "There's something about feeling the hot bubbling water with the cold surrounding air that makes it even more refreshing."

"That, and all these water jets caressing my body," she smiled. "It's like getting a massage from a hundred masseuses."

"You've never enjoyed a hot tub before?" I said, peering at the top of her breasts protruding above the surface of the water as the churning liquid swirled over her erect nipples.

"Not like *this*," she purred, resting her head against her seat rest. "I've had a Jacuzzi bath before, but never outside and never with another person."

I was tempted to tell her about the secret location in the tub where she could receive special stimulation on a different part of her body, but I figured I'd let her discover that for herself another day. It was still early in our relationship, and I didn't want to overstep my role as her host.

"So what do you think of America after your first two days?" I said, changing the subject.

"You mean besides how cold it is in the winter?" she chuckled.

"Sorry about that," I said. "Perhaps you should have looked to relocate to a warmer state like Florida or California."

"Something tells me I'm going to warm up to this place pretty quickly," she said, glancing down at my breasts bobbing atop the swirling water. "Besides, I kind of like the cold weather. My family takes frequent ski trips to the Swiss alps. I don't imagine there's much skiing in Florida or California."

"Florida, no. But you'd be surprised how many ski resorts there are in California. The Sierras get a fair amount of snow in the higher elevations."

"Are there any ski hills near Chicago?"

"There's a few resorts in northern Wisconsin about four hours from here. It's a far cry from the Swiss Alps, but they have passable trails for an intermediate skier."

"I never even thought about bringing my gear with me," Luna said, shaking her head.

"Do you prefer to ski or snowboard?"

"I'm proficient at both, but I'm a slightly better skier."

"Not to worry," I said. "We can rent some equipment at the slopes. Once you get settled in at your new school, we'll make a weekend excursion soon."

"I'd enjoy that very much," Luna nodded, adjusting her position under the swirling water.

"Are you nervous about moving to a new school tomorrow?" I asked.

"Not too much," she said. "I've managed to maintain fairly good grades, and the curriculum between the two school systems is pretty well aligned, so hopefully it won't be too much of any adjustment."

I noticed Luna spreading her arms out to her sides, searching for the new locations of the underwater jets. As she squirmed in her seat, I could tell she was curious to see what they might feel like on other parts of her body, but she was too shy to make such a bold move in my company.

"What about socially?" I asked, eager to see if she had a boyfriend. "Do you make new friends easily?"

"It usually takes me a while to form those kind of bonds," she frowned. "Transferring in the middle of the school year doesn't help."

"Well, I'm sure with your pretty looks and charming French accent that it won't take long for you to find new friends." Then I looked at her with an arched eyebrow and a slight curl of my lip. "Is there a special someone back home that you'll miss *especially* much?"

"Not really," Luna smiled, understanding my meaning immediately. "I've been so focused on my studies trying to make sure I get into a good university. I don't have any time for boyfriends."

My pussy twitched when I heard she was unattached. Suddenly, *I* was the one shifting uneasily under the churning water, desperate to feel the jets pulsing against my pussy as I peered at the pretty French girl.

❧

Later that evening while Luna checked in with her family back home, I went to my bedroom and propped up my pillows, picking up a book from my nightstand. About a half hour later, I heard her run a bath, and I wondered why she needed to bathe again so soon after our long hot tub. Listening to the sound of her body rubbing against the metal tub while she lowered herself into the water, my mind soon drifted away from the book, imagining what she looked like naked.

I wondered if it was true what they said about French girls not shaving their private areas, and I couldn't stop picturing her pretty tits floating atop the clear water. As much as I enjoyed watching her undulate in the frothy water of the hot tub, I would have killed to be in the bathtub with her right now. After a few minutes, I heard a scraping sound like she was shaving her legs, and I smiled.

So much for European girls going au naturel, I thought. *Apparently, they're just as obsessed as American girls about maintaining their smooth skin.*

I found myself holding my breath as I strained to listen to the sound of the razor scraping her skin and the water sloshing over her naked body as she shifted her position periodically in the tub. After a while, the scraping sound stopped and for a while I couldn't hear anything in the washroom. Then I slowly began to hear the sound of ripples lapping against the side of the tub, and I wondered what she was doing. Straining to listen, I heard her begin to mew as the sound of rippling water began to escalate in pitch and frequency.

Is she...? I thought, suddenly sitting up in my bed.

As her breathing and soft moaning began to grow more noticeable, there was no longer any doubt. She was masturbating in the bathtub!

Now I knew why she wanted to take a bath so soon after our hot tub together. She'd apparently gotten just as aroused as me feeling the swirling water jets caressing her body, and she wanted to re-experience the feeling in the privacy of her own room. I wondered if part of it might *also* have to do with a similarly strong attraction she was feeling for me.

I tiptoed across my carpet and opened my door as wide as it would go, then ripped off my clothes, sitting spread-eagled on my bedspread. As I listened to her soft sighs and moans, I placed my fingers against my clit, surprised at how wet I'd gotten in the last few minutes. While the pleasurable sensations began to spread throughout my body, I closed my eyes imagining what she looked like as she touched herself in the bathtub.

Did she like to squeeze her tits like me when she played with her clit? Did she like to place two fingers inside her pussy and stimulate her G-spot while rubbing her palm against her vulva? Did she have one leg propped up on the side of the bathtub while she jilled herself spread-eagled in the sudsy water? I could almost see the flush spreading over her chest and cheeks as her pleasure escalated in intensity. It didn't take long for the image I was cultivating in my mind to get me so worked up that I experienced a sudden orgasm, squealing softly as I bit my lip.

Suddenly the sloshing sound in the bathroom stopped for a moment as Luna paused to hear what I was doing. While I lay on the bed motionless with my fingers still embedded in my pussy, I felt my heart pounding in my chest as I struggled to slow my breath so Luna wouldn't know what I'd been secretly doing while she touched herself. Then a few moments later, the rhythmic sloshing sound resumed and I heard her moaning and sighing as her body squeaked against the slippery metal surface of the tub.

This time, I remained perfectly still while I curled my fingers softly inside my pussy, listening to Luna's breathing and groans growing more pronounced. Suddenly, I heard a loud splash as she jerked her body forcefully in the tub, and I knew that she'd reached orgasm. Consumed with desire, I began pounding my fingers in and out of my pussy while I tribbed my burning clit with the fingers of my other hand.

This time, my orgasm washed over me like a freight train, and I arched my hips high off the bed, gaping my mouth wide open in the throes of a powerful climax. Trying to stifle my moans, I held my body in an arched position for almost thirty seconds as wave after wave of intense contractions rolled over my body. When I finally collapsed onto my bed, the springs squeaked loudly, and the house became eerily silent.

I wondered if Luna sensed that I'd been pleasuring myself while I listened to her, just as she'd done with me. Either way, something told me there'd be a lot more than just *studying* going on in my household over the next four or five months.

4

———

For the next few weeks, things quieted down as Luna settled in to her new school and concentrated on her studies. We went shopping on weekends, watched movies together on the sofa on weeknights, and enjoyed frequent hot tub dips. But as much as I sensed the burgeoning sexual tension between the two of us, neither of us felt brave enough to make the first move for fear of breaking our unwritten host-student pact.

With the mid-winter school break approaching, I asked Luna if she wanted to head north for a few days of skiing. When she quickly agreed, I booked three nights at a cozy hotel near Granite Peak at Rib Mountain State Park. Luna was an excellent skier, and I had a hard time keeping up with her down the mogul-covered expert trails. In the evenings, we went out for dinner at local restaurants and by the time we returned to the hotel, we were both so exhausted, we fell asleep before ten p.m. But I saw enough of her in her skimpy underwear to have vivid dreams fantasizing about pouncing on top of her on the adjacent bed in our single hotel room. By the time we headed back home, I felt our relationship had reached a new level of comfort and closeness.

"Did you enjoy our little getaway?" I said, peering over at Luna as she stared out her window on the drive home.

"Yes, thank you so much, Jade," she said, turning to face me with a big smile. "You're the best host I could have ever hoped for. Sometimes I feel like I've hardly left home. Between the ski trips, restaurants, shopping, and everything else, you've made me feel like part of your family."

"Everything but the *hot tubs*, right?" I grinned.

"I have to admit, that's a lovely perk," she nodded. "Although with the weather beginning to warm up, we might not have so much need for it soon."

"In another month or so we can look into opening up the pool. It's heated too, so maybe you'll find it just as relaxing and refreshing on cool evenings and weekends."

"I'll have to look into getting my own swim suit soon," she smiled. "I'm going to wear yours out pretty soon with all the use it gets in the hot tub."

"Now that you *mention* that," I said, peering over at her. "I've been thinking. You've told me about your dressmaking hobby and your interest in exploring fashion design as a potential career. I'd like to buy you a sewing machine so you'll have something else to do with your free time."

"I could never expect you to buy me such an expensive gift," Luna said, shaking her head. "You've already spent far too much paying for the hotel and the restaurants on this ski trip."

"Hey, I enjoyed those just as much as *you* did. Besides, I've been wanting to get a sewing machine for myself for some time now. They're not that expensive, and I'll get almost as much use out of it after you've gone as you will."

"Only if you *promise* to use it after I leave," Luna said, peering at me earnestly. Then her expression changed as her eyes opened wide and her forehead wrinkled in delight. "Maybe we can have some fun designing and making patterns *together*!"

"I'd really enjoy that, Luna. We still have a few days left in the winter holiday. Would you like to go to the fabric store tomorrow and look around for ideas?"

"That would be awesome!" Luna said, bouncing up and down excitedly on her car seat. "Oh my God–you're the *best*, Jade!"

The following day, we set out to the local fabric store to begin searching for material. We both agreed that we'd like to surprise each other with our initial designs, so we paid for our samples separately then we went home and began sketching some ideas. After supplying each other with our measurements, we set out crafting our garments. With Luna's measurements of 35-23-34, I wanted to make something sexy and flattering for her figure. While *she* worked in the evenings and on weekends on her design, I worked during the day while she was at school.

When the day finally came to reveal our designs to each other, we met in the living room like two kids at Christmas. We did rock-paper-scissors to see who would go first, and Luna won the first round.

"Okay," she said excitedly to me. "I've got your item wrapped up in this garment bag, so I want you to turn around before I reveal it."

"Now you've got *me* all excited," I said, turning around to face the windows looking out into the backyard. "Tell me when it's okay to turn around."

I heard Luna unzip her garment bag, followed by a slight rustling sound, then she giggled softly.

"Okay, I'm ready," she said.

I turned around and peered at a cream-colored linen mid-length dress with cropped sleeves and a small slit on each side of the lower hem.

"Wow," I said, widening my eyes. "It looks *gorgeous*! Can I try it on?"

"Absolutely," Luna smiled with a huge grin.

"Do you mind if I undress here?"

"It's just us girls," she nodded with a smile. "No one else is looking."

I kicked off my loafers then pulled my pants down and unzipped my blouse, laying them over the back edge of the sofa. Then I unzipped the back closure and stepped into the dress wearing only a bra and panties. The dress fit snuggly over my hips and ass, and the V-neck top hugged my bosom perfectly, creating a slim, tapered look.

"Can you zip me up in the back?" I said, turning around.

For the first time, I felt Luna's hands caress my bare skin as she closed the panels and zipped them together. I turned around to face her, feeling my nipples getting hard and my panties moistening.

"It fits perfectly," I gushed, swiping my hands down the side of the dress, stepping forward to see how much room I had to maneuver. "And the little side slits leave just enough room to move around comfortably. You absolutely *nailed* this one, Luna. How did you know linen was one of my favorite fabrics?"

Luna looked at me sheepishly and shrugged.

"I confess that I peeked in your closet when you weren't looking to get some ideas. I hope you like it."

"I love it!" I said. "It's classic, sexy, and timeless. Though I might not be able to wear it until summer. Because of that silly no-white-before-Memorial-Day rule."

"At least I'll see it on you before I leave," Luna smiled. "I was hoping you might also wear it when you come to visit me in France this summer."

"I'd love that Luna," I smiled, leaning in to kiss her on the cheek.

"Why don't you go for a walk down the hall to see how comfortably it moves with you?"

"Okay," I said, strutting down the hall using my best supermodel catwalk imitation, swinging my hips from side to side in an exaggerated manner as I stepped one foot in front of the other.

"Wow," Luna said. "It almost looks better from *behind* than from the front, if you don't mind my saying. Is there enough room for you to walk comfortably?"

"Absolutely," I said, swinging around and affecting a pouty model face as I strode back down the hall toward her. "There's just enough play in the skirt with the side slits to allow me to walk with a normal gait. This is the absolute perfect dress! Thank you, Luna, for making me such a pretty garment. You really do have a knack for this."

"The pleasure was all mine," Luna beamed. "But with a figure like yours, I suspect even a *potato sack* would look good on you."

"Hardly," I said. "But it's my turn now. Turn around while I get your surprise ready."

"Okay," Luna squeaked, barely able to contain herself as she turned to face the windows overlooking the backyard.

I pulled her two-piece garment out of a department store bag and held them up, one on top of the other.

"Okay," I said, excited to reveal my design. "You can turn around now."

When Luna flipped around and saw what I'd made, her eyes flew open and she jumped up and down excitedly.

"Oh my God—they're *beautiful!*" she exclaimed, moving in closer to examine the lacy camisole and matching silk shorts.

"I hope you don't think I was being too forward designing a sexy loungewear set for you," I said. "But I thought these would look beautiful on you and now that you're almost finished high school, I thought you might like something to make you feel all grown up."

"Are you *kidding* me?" she said. "I've always dreamed of owning something like this, but my parents would never let me wear them."

She stepped forward and pinched the fabric between her fingers, rubbing it softly.

"Is this...?"

"Yes," I smiled. "It's real silk. None of that fake polyester Victoria's Secret stuff for my pretty European model. I wanted to make a first-class outfit for a first-class girl."

"Can I try them on?" she said.

"Of course. That is, if you feel comfortable taking your clothes off—"

Luna practically ripped off her jeans and t-shirt then unclasped her bra and pulled down her panties, throwing them in a pile next to mine on the sofa. Seeing her for the first time naked, I couldn't help but glance down at her exquisite figure. Her breasts sat high and proud on her chest, pointing straight out like a Madonna corset, with large brown areolas and pink nubs. Her mound was shaved perfectly bald, and my mind suddenly wandered back to the memory of listening to her shaving in the bathtub while my pussy fluttered under my linen dress.

She pulled on the silky shorts first, then she lifted her arms as I watched the camisole slide down over her shoulders and her protruding tits. I was worried about getting the fit right over her uniquely shaped breasts, but when the straps fell over her shoulders, the fabric draped sexily over her mounds with just the right amount of cling and loose folds. And the lacy top hem swept down just enough to tastefully show off her tight cleavage without making it look trampy.

"How do I look?" Luna said, smiling at me sexily.

"*Mouth-watering*," I said, feeling my panties growing damper by the moment. "You could give any one of those Victoria Secret models a run for their money. How's the fit?"

"It clings to my body with just the right amount of drape. And the silk feels absolutely heavenly against my bare skin. Do you mind if I see what it looks like in your upstairs dressing mirror?"

"Of course," I said, taking her hand and leading her toward the stairs. "I was thinking the same thing."

When we got to my bedroom, Luna stepped in front of the full-length mirror and gasped. The soft baby-blue with cream-colored lace accents made her look sexy and innocent at the same time. While she peered at the front profile of her lingerie set, I ran my eyes over her tight ass perfectly framed by the clingy silk fabric.

"It fits me perfectly!" she gushed, twisting her body from side to side while she peered at herself in front of the mirror. "How does it look from behind?"

"Just as sexy as from the *front*," I smiled. "See for yourself."

Luna turned her body around then twisted her head to look at her reflection in the mirror.

"How did you get it to fit me so perfectly?" she said, pushing her butt out in a vampy pose. "It fits every curve of my body like a glove!"

"I've had a fair amount of time to study your body in my wet swimsuit in the hot tub these past few weeks. Your figure is indelibly imprinted on my brain."

"Thank you, Jade," Luna said, rushing up toward me and flinging her arms around my neck while she pressed her tits and hips against me.

As I hugged her softly, I desperately wanted to place my hand under her chin and kiss her, pulling her onto the bed only a few inches away. But somehow I managed to keep it together and release her after a few moments, while we continued admiring our fashion designs in the mirror.

If this was the best way to get her body pressing up against mine, I thought, I was already thinking of the *next* clothing design I had in mind for her.

5

Over the next few weeks, Luna and I continued to make increasingly sexy outfits for one another. My next design was a cut-out one-piece swimsuit with a large oval opening on both sides of her midsection that accentuated her curvy figure. For her part, she designed a matching lace bra and panty ensemble that took my lingerie set one step further. Feeling excited about carrying our mutual clothing design venture to the next level, I left a message for her on the fridge one afternoon while I went to the fabric store to shop for more material.

Luna,

    Running some errands this afternoon. Should be home around 5:00 p.m. Feel like pizza tonight?

    Jade

I received a text back from her when she got home from school saying pizza sounded great, but by then I'd finished most of my shopping so I headed back a bit earlier than planned. When I pulled into the driveway, I didn't open the garage door like usual because I wanted to sneak my new fabric design in without her seeing it.

Opening the door softly, I tiptoed down the hall and up the stairs, hoping to hide the material in my closet.

But as I approached my bedroom, I heard a soft buzzing sound and I paused at the partially closed door, peering through the crack. Luna was lying buck naked on my bed with a vibrator humming loudly between her legs. I recognized it immediately as my Rabbit vibrator and she was holding the end of it with two hands while she pressed the flapping ears tightly against her pussy.

Instantly aroused in a fit of passion, I placed the fabric bag down on the floor and unzipped my pants, thrusting my fingers under my soaking panties. As I watched Luna ramming the dildo in and out of her bare cunny, I trilled my clit rapidly, feeling my knees beginning to weaken. She looked even *more* beautiful with a soft flush filling her face and her pointy tits jiggling on her chest as she rolled her hips and flexed her arms, fucking herself with the buzzing vibrator.

As she began to arch her back and widen her mouth in mounting ecstasy, it took every ounce of my willpower not to barge through the door and take her into my arms. The more she tensed her body and arched her back, the closer my own orgasm steamrolled toward me. When she suddenly grunted and began jerking her body forward and back in the midst of a powerful orgasm, I felt my juices spraying all over my hand and jeans resting halfway down my thighs.

I was tempted to sneak away before she caught me lurking outside the door, but there was something about seeing the girl I'd fantasized about for the past two months naked on my bed that kept me hesitating in the hall. After she recovered from her orgasm, she pulled the still-buzzing Rabbit vibrator out of her pussy. Seeing her juices glistening on the whirring contraption made my pussy throb as two more steams of lubrication trickled down the inside of my thighs. When she reached over and pulled open my nightstand drawer to search for another toy, I smiled.

That's it, baby, I purred. *Go ahead and try out my entire collection. Give your momma a nice show.*

When she lifted the oversize Magic Wand vibrator out of the drawer, my heart fluttered.

You better be careful with that one, sweetie. It packs a hellova punch.

This was one of the few vibrators I owned that had a power cord, and Luna lifted herself off the bed, searching for the nearest outlet. While I watched her bend over, revealing the glistening slit between her legs as she plugged the device into the wall, I kicked off my jeans and panties, eager to free up my pussy for less restricted access. Something told me this show might go on for a while, and I planned on enjoying it to the fullest. But when she climbed back on the bed instead of lying back down face up, she surprised me by getting on all fours with her bare ass pointed directly in my direction.

Fuck me, I thought to myself. *You're making this damn near impossible for me, girl.* Now it was going to be even more difficult to restrain myself from barging through the door and pouncing on top of her.

As I watched her spread her knees apart then rest her chest on the bed as she angled her hips up in the air, I stood mesmerized outside the door. I could see her entire gleaming vulva from her bald pubis down over her splayed lips, all the way to her tight brown pucker. Even her swollen clit was visible from my position, poised like a ripe cherry at the junction of her folds under the bottom of her mound.

Oh, how I longed to be lying between her legs, taking her plump fruit into my mouth.

But when she flicked on the big vibrator and positioned the pulsating ball over her erect gland, I lost all sense of space and time. As her hips began to undulate against the vibrating head, I thrust three fingers inside my pussy and began fucking myself hard. I could see her tits hanging between the A-frame of her splayed legs, and when she grabbed one breast with her other hand and began squeezing it while she moaned in pleasure, I unbuttoned my own blouse and thrust my bra up under my neck, pinching my nipples.

I hadn't witnessed such an erotic sight in a very long time, and I bit my lip trying to remain silent while I watched the sexy nymph pleasuring herself. As I watched her juices pouring out of her snatch and rolling down the insides of her thighs, I could hear her cries and whimpers growing in urgency. But when she reached around behind her ass with her free hand and thrust two fingers into her pussy while she rocked back and forth on the bed, I almost lost it. I had to stop fingering myself for fear of falling off the cliff and making a commotion.

Besides, I wanted to save myself for the big finish. I wanted to dream that I was right there *with* her, grinding my sopping pussy against her while we came together.

As Luna began pumping her fingers harder into her hole, she turned her head sideways on the bed, and I saw the look of ecstasy on her face. As she opened her mouth wider approaching another orgasm, I suddenly felt my cunt clamping down on my fingers as I jetted my juices all over my palm. Seconds later, Luna emitted a loud squeal as she pulled her fingers out of her cunny and I saw her rosebud contracting in powerful convulsions while she pressed the vibrating ball of the magic wand hard against the base of her mound.

Oh my God, I panted outside my door, trying to control my breathing so as not to be heard.

Thinking that would be the end of it, I was surprised a few minutes later when Luna peered inside the drawer one more time then pulled out my favorite sex toy, the Osé vibrator. Designed to mimic the movement of a person's natural anatomy, the uniquely shaped device had a long bulbous finger-shaped projection that curled forward in rhythmic pulses to stimulate the front side of a woman's G-spot. The other part of the device had a small opening in the base with a flexible tongue designed to imitate the action of a person's mouth. When it was fully inserted into the vagina, the two parts together delivered an unforgettable experience unlike anything else, designed to give its recipient a blended, full-body orgasm.

Luna peered at the device with pinched eyebrows for a moment, turning it over in her hands trying to figure out how the various parts worked. Eventually, she found the power button on the base of the unit, and when she held it down I saw a small green LED light illuminate.

That's my girl, I smiled. *It takes a little getting used to, but if you just play with the buttons enough, you'll figure it out.*

Flipping the device upside-down, she noticed the control buttons under the base. She pressed one of the buttons, then her eyes lit up as the finger-shaped appendage began flexing toward her in a come-hither motion. When she pressed the little plus symbol next to the button, the finger began moving more rapidly. Shaking her head in shock, she ramped down the speed of the finger then tapped the other button. Suddenly, the aperture at the base of the unit began to pucker open and shut, mimicking the motion of a moving mouth. Luna leaned her head closer to the device, mesmerized by the strange object.

Pretty incredible, right? I muttered, teleporting my thoughts to her through the thin crack in the door. *You have no idea how heavenly it feels until you actually put it inside you.*

She turned all the power functions off, then sat up against my headboard with her knees hiked up toward her chest. Then she slowly inserted the long finger into her slit until the base was pressed firmly against her vulva. When she tapped the finger-control button on the base of the unit and felt it moving inside her, she groaned softly.

"Yes, Jade," she purred. "Finger my pussy while I look at your beautiful body."

I stepped away from the door, wondering if she'd seen my shadow moving in the hall. But when I peered back at her, her eyes were closed as she continued talking to herself. When she tapped the clitoral-control button, she slid her hips down while spreading her knees further apart.

"Oh God, Jade," she moaned. "That feels incredible. Lick my clit with your soft tongue. I want to feel your face against my pussy when I come."

Holy shit, I thought, plunging my fingers back into my dripping hole. *She's fantasizing about the device being my own fingers and mouth touching her instead of the artificial toy!*

Knowing she wanted me as much as I'd fantasized about having her, ratcheted up my pleasure tenfold as my juices began flowing out of my pussy in rivers. I was tempted to swing open the door and tell her I was waiting right here for her, but I didn't want to invade her privacy and embarrass her using my toys. I'd have to wait for another time to make my first move. But right now, I was going to *enjoy* this fantasy show to the fullest.

As she began to undulate her hips against the throbbing device, Luna tapped the plus button on the base of the unit, increasing the speed and intensity of the two simultaneous functions. Holding the base of the unit tightly against her snatch, she grabbed one of her tits with her other hand and moaned loudly.

"Fuck yes," she grunted. "Suck my clit while you finger my cunt, Jade. You feel so good, I'm going to come soon all over your face..."

Yes please, I hissed, watching her fuck herself with the animatronic device. My juices were now dripping all over my hand and my pants lying on the floor below my legs, and I wondered how I was going to put them back on and sneak past her without her knowing what I'd been doing.

"Jade!" she suddenly squealed. "I'm going to come. I'm going to come so hard all over your pretty face. Make me–*unghhh!*"

When I saw Luna climaxing again with the sexy toy embedded in her pussy, I watched her face contorted in sweet agony, wishing it was my face planted between her knees instead of the artificial vibrator. As her body quivered and writhed on the bed in the midst of another powerful climax, I clenched my jaw trying to control my breathing, pursing my lips to make sure she couldn't hear my own suppressed squeaks. It was most powerful orgasm I'd experienced in months, and it took almost a full minute for my contractions to stop pulsing inside me.

When I finally stopped shaking outside the door, Luna suddenly turned her wrist to look at her watch, then she got up off the bed and dashed into the washroom to clean off the vibrators. I looked at my phone, and realizing it was approaching five o'clock, I pulled up my pants and crept back downstairs. Then I quietly opened the front door and waited outside on the doorstep for a few minutes to allow Luna to put herself back together.

After three or four minutes, I opened the door with a flourish and called Luna's name to announce myself.

"Hello beautiful," I shouted. "I'm home. Are you hungry?"

I smiled listening to her scampering upstairs as she ran from my bedroom into her own. It looked like the two of us were going to continue our little cat-and-mouse game for a little longer. Holding the fabric store shopping bag in front of my crotch as I ascended the stairs to conceal the giant wet stain on the front of my jeans, I scurried into my room and changed into fresh clothes. After I stowed the shopping bag in my closet and washed the smell of my juices off my hands, I went downstairs and saw Luna sitting on the sofa watching TV like nothing had happened.

"How was your day today?" I asked, pressing my lips together to conceal my knowing smile.

"Pretty uneventful," Luna replied. "You?"

"I picked up some more material at the fabric store. I can't wait for you to see what I've got planned for my next surprise."

"I like surprises," Luna said, peering back at me from the sofa.

"Me too," I smiled. "Are you hungry?"

"Voracious," she said. "I could eat a horse."

That's not the only thing I could eat right now, I thought, gazing back at her like a Cheshire Cat.

6

———

For the next week or so, the sexual tension in the house continued to ramp up as Luna took more frequent baths, making little effort to conceal her increasingly noisy self-pleasuring activity. One day, not long after school ended, I came home from a shopping trip and saw her lying in the hot tub with a more flushed face than usual. As I began putting the groceries away in the cupboards, I glanced at her in the reflection of the microwave glass panel and noticed that she was positioned in the special spot where she could receive direct underwater stimulation to her private areas.

I turned around and motioned to her that I was coming out to join her, and she waved for me to come in. But this time, I didn't even bother going through the pretense of changing into a bathing suit as I stripped off my clothes and scampered out the back door, lowering my naked body into the swirling water.

"I hope you don't mind if I enjoy the hot tub in the *nude* this time," I said. "I think we've seen each naked enough times by now that there shouldn't be any more surprises."

"Of course not," she smiled. "I was thinking the same thing.

Though I have to admit I've been enjoying wearing this sexy new swimsuit you made for me."

"Are you finding the openings in the fabric provide enough stimulation from the underwater jets?"

"Yes," she said, subtly adjusting her position on the seat. "Although sometimes I wish there were a few *other* strategically placed holes for me to fully appreciate this experience."

"I know what you mean," I smiled. "I see you've found the special spot in the tub where you can receive an even *more* invigorating massage."

"It's pretty hard to miss," Luna nodded, spreading her legs wider apart under the churning water. "Is there a similar spot on the other side of the tub where you can enjoy it too?"

"As a matter of fact, there *is*," I grinned, positioning my pussy directly in front of the underwater jet shooting up from the base of the tub. "*Mmm*–that feels better."

"You seem to have quite a few toys in the household for stimulating your body," she smiled.

"How do you mean?" I asked coyly. "Like *what* other toys?"

"Um..." Luna hesitated as a deep flush rolled over her face.

"It's okay," I said. "I know that you found my secret stash of sex toys. I saw you using them one day when I came home a bit early."

"You don't mind?"

"Are you kidding me?" I said. "I enjoyed watching you almost as you did *using* them."

"Well now that we're not sharing secrets anymore," Luna smiled. "I heard you out in the hall that day. I enjoyed giving you a little show, hoping you might come in and join me on the bed."

"Oh, Luna," I gushed, feeling the powerful jet spraying against my tingling clit. "I've wanted you from the minute I first saw you–"

"The feeling was mutual," Luna said, looking me squarely in my eyes as her own pleasure beginning to escalate from the jet caressing her covered vulva.

She pulled her hands out of the water and stripped off her swimsuit, throwing it on the deck of the hot tub.

"Fuck it," she said. "No more playing around. I'm going to enjoy this hot tub the way it was intended. I want to come this time watching you orgasm with me."

"Yes, baby," I panted. "Come with me while I watch you. I'm already close."

"I'm coming, Jade," Luna suddenly grunted as her eyes glazed over.

"Uhnnn," I groaned, gazing at her as we both shuddered under the swirling water.

We watched our heads bobbing in spastic union for a few moments, then we both smiled.

"That took a lot longer to happen than I planned," I said.

"Why don't we go upstairs and *finish* this properly?" Luna smiled. "It's about time I felt your soft skin against me instead of these artificial jets or a silicone sex toy."

"Are you sure you want to do this?" I said, hardly believing my own ears. "I mean, we'd be overstepping the bounds of our arrangement..."

"We're both adults," Luna said. "What Ms. Laurent and my parents don't know won't hurt them. I need you so bad. Please make love to me, Jade."

"You're twisting my arm," I said. "But just to be sure the neighbors don't get suspicious, why don't you put your swimsuit back on before you get out of the tub? I'll join you in a few minutes after I make sure the coast is clear."

"Good idea," Luna said, pulling the suit off the deck and squeezing her body back into it under the cover of the water. "I'll be waiting for you in your bed upstairs."

The next two minutes seemed like an eternity as I thought about my sexy angel waiting for me naked and dripping wet. After a short waiting period, I glanced around me at the surrounding yards to make sure nobody was watching, then I scampered out of the hot tub and ran upstairs, not even bothering to dry off. When I saw Luna spread out naked on my bed with the covers pulled down, I jumped on the mattress next to her, wrapping my arms and legs tightly around her.

"Luna," I panted, feeling electrified from the sensation of her warm body next to mine. "I can't believe we're finally going to do this. I've waited so long..."

"Me too," Luna purred, pressing her hips and breasts against mine. "I always wondered what it would be like to make love to a woman. And I can't imagine a more perfect partner. I've grown very close to you these past few months."

"Oh baby," I sighed. "I feel exactly the same way. I haven't felt like this in such a long time."

"Is this your first time with a woman also?" she asked.

"No," I smiled. "But it's the first time with another woman I've felt so close to."

"Make love to me, Jade," she purred. "I want to feel your love as you caress me."

"Yes, baby," I said. "I'm going to love every square inch of your body."

I inserted my thigh between her legs and pulled it up toward her crotch, feeling her slippery lubrication coating the inside of her thighs. When I pressed my leg against her pussy, she moaned, thrusting her tongue into my mouth while we kissed each other passionately.

"Mmm," she hummed. "You feel so soft. I want to feel you *everywhere*."

"Oh you *will* baby," I said, edging myself lower down her body.

When I reached her neck, I nibbled on her skin then sucked her flesh into my mouth.

"I thought we were supposed to be careful about letting people know what we've been up to?" she said. "You're going to leave hickeys all over me!"

"Who's to say they were from *me*?" I smiled. "You're a big girl now. Isn't this what teenagers do to each other behind the portables at school?"

"You're very bad, Jade," Luna panted.

"You have *no* idea," I said.

Feeling her tits caressing the sides of my neck, I moved my face lower, swirling my tongue over her beautiful brown medallions while I sucked her erect nipples into my mouth with a loud popping sound. I'd dreamed of sucking her tits ever since I saw her in her tight sweater. Feeling her finally in my soft, pliant mouth was driving me insane with desire, and I could feel my juices coating her thighs as I rubbed my body against her. I lifted my face and squeezed her tits with my hands, kneading the firm flesh between my fingers.

"You have no idea how much I've wanted to touch you like this," I said, blowing softly on her puckering teats.

"Oh, I have an idea," she groaned. "Between the sexy lingerie set you designed for me and the cutaway swimsuit, you seemed to be overly focused on my girl parts."

"You got that right," I said. "Do you mind if I take a moment to fulfill one particular fantasy I've been harboring ever since I saw these beautiful breasts up close and personal?"

"I can't imagine what you're thinking," Luna smiled. "But I want you to do everything a woman can do to another woman in the remaining time we have together. I don't ever want to forget this time we have left."

I lifted my body up and knelt over her torso with my knees straddling her chest, then I lowered my dripping pussy onto one of her tits. When she felt my warm vulva touching her skin, she reached down and grabbed her breast with two hands, rolling it back and forth over my throbbing slit.

"Oh *God*, Luna," I panted, feeling her erect nipple pressing into my opening. "Fuck me with your beautiful breasts. That feels incredible."

"This is way better than playing with a *sex toy*," she said, smiling up at me.

"Even that special *white* one with the bendy finger and realistic tongue action?"

"There's no comparison," she said. "You're softer, warmer, and wetter. And besides, you can't make *love* to a sex toy, even one that imitates human movement so well."

"Oh, Luna," I said, bending forward to kiss her. "I've fallen in love with you these past few months. I don't ever want you to leave."

"Let's enjoy the little time we have together to the fullest," she smiled. "We have a lot of catching up to do."

"Mmm," I said, rolling my sopping pussy all over her firm mounds. "You feel so good, baby. Keep tribbing me with your tits."

As Luna flapped her breast against my quivering pussy, I moaned louder and louder into her mouth, rapidly approaching my peak. Sensing I was getting close, Luna grabbed the sides of my hips, slowing my movement.

"Can I feel you come in my *mouth* instead this first time?" she asked. "I want to watch your face while I kiss you in your most intimate place. This has been *my* fantasy these past few months."

"As long as you let me return the favor," I said, lifting my head and gazing into her eyes. "Are you sure you're going to know how to do this?"

"How hard can it be?" she smiled. "I'll just imitate the action of the Osé sex toy that I used while you were watching me a few days ago."

"Mmm," I nodded. "I've come many times imagining that was another woman's mouth on my pussy. But something tells me this time it's going to be a hundred times better."

"Only a *hundred*?" Luna smirked.

"Come here," I said, shimmying my hips overtop of her head and lowering my steaming cunt onto her rosebud lips. "Suck my pussy with those pretty lips."

"Mmmm," Luna moaned, feeling my erect nub in her mouth as I coated her face with the juices streaming out of my slit.

She looked up at me and grabbed both of my tits with her two hands, squeezing them firmly. Seeing her pretty face framed by my thighs straddling her head drove me crazy, and when we locked eyes expressing how close we felt to one another at that moment, a tear rolled down my cheek.

"Luna," I groaned. "I love you, baby. It won't take me long now. Can I come on your sweet, beautiful face?"

"*Mm-hmm*," Luna nodded excitedly, squeezing my tits with three quick pulses to show that she returned the sentiment.

"Here's it comes, baby," I gushed. "Oh God, I'm *cumming. Nnngh!*"

As my orgasm washed over me, my entire body began shaking as I gushed all over Luna's flushed cheeks. She blinked her eyes in surprise but never stopped caressing my clit as she sucked it tightly in her mouth. While I sat convulsing over her face, she peered up at me with her aquamarine eyes, cupping my breasts lovingly in her hands. When I finally finished coming, I lifted myself off her and lay down next to her, tasting my juices on her lips as I intertwined my tongue with hers.

"That was *incredible*," I said, pulling back to look into her eyes.

"Was I okay for my first time?"

"*Okay*?" I said, widening my eyes. "You're a natural at this. Now I'm going to miss you all the more when you leave. Nothing's going to make up for you being gone."

"Not even that special rabbit vibrator with the rotating shaft and the flapping ears?"

"Not even *that*," I laughed, leaning in to kiss her again. "But it's your turn now. I've been dreaming about touching *another* part of your body for quite a while. It's time for me to taste *you* and feel you come in my mouth now."

"I'd like that," Luna smiled. "But we've still got a few days to explore each other's bodies. Can you *hold* me when you make love to me this time? I want to feel *every* part of you rubbing up against me when we come together."

"*God* yes," I said. "You've been reading my mind."

I rolled Luna onto her back then lifted myself on top of her, straightening my legs between hers as I pressed my pubis against her mound. She lifted her knees and spread her legs apart as she angled her hips upward, pressing her wet vulva against mine. We both moaned and grabbed each other's heads, pulling our lips together. As our tongues danced in each other's mouths, we began to rock our hips in unison. I could feel Luna's tits pressing against mine, and my entire body tingled from the sensation of her rubbing up against me.

She rocked her hips awkwardly against mine, trying to lock our pussies together, but in our missionary position it was difficult to get traction on both of our clits. I lifted my body and moved up a few inches, straddling her stomach with my thighs, then I pressed my sex down over her bald mound. She spread her legs further apart at the same time, tilting her hips upward until our glands touched. When she felt my hard clit rubbing against hers, she groaned deeply into my mouth, pressing her fingers into my back.

As we began to hump each other, I could hear the sound of our wet pussies smacking together while our juices rolled down the insides of both our thighs. Feeling her warm flesh pressed against mine was everything I'd dreamed of, and it didn't take long for me to feel the familiar pangs of a powerful orgasm rising within me again.

"Luna," I panted. "I've wanted to feel you like this for so long. I'm going to come soon. Let me feel you come *with* me while I hold you in my arms."

"Yes, Jade," Luna grunted. "I feel so close to you. Oh *God*!"

Suddenly she dug her nails hard into my back as she squeezed my hips tightly with her thighs, grunting loudly into my mouth. Feeling her hot pussy against mine when she came soon pushed me also over the edge also, as I sprayed my juices all over her gaping hole while I pressed my cunt hard against her. As we both squealed and groaned into each other's mouths, I held her tightly until we finished coming. When we finally finished quivering in each other's arms, I lay down beside her, softly stroking her cheek as I gazed into her eyes.

"Do you know what we French girls call an orgasm?" she said, smiling at me.

"I have no idea," I said, shaking my head.

"We call it *la petite mort*," she said. "It means little death."

"That's funny," I chuckled. "I guess that's kind of fitting, given all the convulsions we experience at the moment of climax and the way we go limp afterwards. But that reminds me. I haven't spent nearly as much time as I'd hoped learning your language while you've been with me. There's so much more I was hoping you could teach me."

"I'll be happy to," Luna said, suddenly rolling back on top of me. "But something tells me you've still got plenty to teach me too."

As our bodies melded back together again, I couldn't help smiling. This cultural exchange program had been far more beneficial for both of us than I'd ever imagined.

R*eady for more erotic chills and thrills? Enjoy the next volume in* the Erotica Themed Bundles series, *All Girl 6. Buy direct and save at victoriarusherotica. Or download from your favorite online bookstore here:* retailer links.

Only a woman really knows how to satisfy another woman...

ALSO BY VICTORIA RUSH

Adult Fairytales:

The Enchanted Forest: An Erotic Fairytale

The Land of Giants: An Erotic Fairytale

The Dragon's Lair: An Erotic Fairytale

Witch's Brew: An Erotic Fairytale

The Mage's Spell: An Erotic Fairytale

The Mermaid Lagoon: An Erotic Fairytale

The Coven: An Erotic Fairytale

Rapunzel: An Erotic Fairytale

The Seven Dwarfs: An Erotic Fairytale

The Land of Mutants: An Erotic Fairytale

The Erotic Temple: A Sexy Fairytale (Coming Soon)

Erotica Themed Bundles:

Voyeur: Lesbian Erotica Bundle

Public Affairs: A Lesbian Anthology

Futa Fantasies: The Ladyboy Collection

Threesomes: The Lesbian Collection

Threesomes - Volume 2: The Lesbian Collection

First Time: A Lesbian Anthology

Hedonism: An Erotic Anthology

Switch Hitters: Bisexual Erotica

Taboo Erotica: The Lesbian Series

BDSM: The Lesbian Collection

Party Games: The Erotic Collection

Party Games 2: The Erotic Collection

All Girl 1: Lesbian Erotica Bundle

All Girl 2: Lesbian Erotica Bundle

All Girl 3: Lesbian Erotica Bundle

All Girl 4: Lesbian Erotica Bundle

Erotic Fairytale Bundles:

Clover's Fantasy Adventures: Books 1 - 5

Clover's Fantasy Adventures: Books 6 - 10

Erotic Fantasy:

Pirate's Bounty: A Time Travel Adventure

Wild West: A Time Travel Adventure

Private Riley: A Time Travel Adventure

Cleopatra's Secret: A Time Travel Adventure

Bounty Hunter 2125: A Time Travel Adventure

Ninja Assassin: A Time Travel Adventure

The 300: A Time Travel Adventure

Arabian Nights: An Erotic Fairytale (coming soon...)

Steamy Time Travel Bundles:

Riley's Time Travel Adventures: Books 1 - 5

Lesbian Erotica:

The Dinner Party: Lesbian Voyeur Erotica

The Darkroom: Bisexual Voyeur Erotica

Naked Yoga: Lesbian Transgender Erotica

Nude Cruise: Bisexual Voyeur Erotica

Rush Hour: Taboo Public Sex

The Girl Next Door: First Time Lesbian Erotic Romance

Girls' Camp: Lesbian Group Sex

Wet Dream: Ladyboy Fantasy Erotica

The Convent: Taboo Sex with a Nun

Sex Robot: A Dream Sex Machine

The Personal Trainer: Getting Pumped at the Gym

The Dominatrix: BDSM Lesbian Domination

Webcam Chat: Lesbian Online Sex

Paint Me: A Kinky Bodypainting Workshop

The Toy Party: Girls Sharing Sex Toys

The Costume Party: Strapping One On

Swedish Sauna: Lesbian Group Sex

The Therapist: Taboo Lesbian Erotica

Elevator Shaft: Bisexual Threesomes Erotica

Ladyboy: Lesbian Transgender Erotica

Peep Show: Lesbian Voyeur Erotica

The Dare: Public Sex Erotica

Maid Service: Lesbian Threesomes Erotica

The Hitchhiker: First Time Lesbian Erotica

The Housesitter: Spycam Lesbian Erotica

The Spa: Lesbian Group Orgy

Parlor Games: Blindfold Sex Party

The Exchange Student: First Time Lesbian Erotica

The Hostel: Bisexual Group Erotica

The Harem: Lesbian Erotic Romance

The Orient Express: Lesbian Voyeur Erotica

The First Lady: A Forbidden Lesbian Erotic Romance

The Slave: Lesbian BDSM Erotica

The Masseuse: Lesbian Sensuous Erotica

Too Close for Comfort: Lesbian Forbidden Erotica

Naked Twister: A Wild Party Game

Lexi: The Sex App (Lesbian Fantasy Erotica)

Call Girl: Lesbian Bisexual Threesomes Erotica

Circle Jill: Lesbian Masturbation Workshop

The Viewing Room: Masturbation Voyeur Erotica

Spin the Bottle: A Kinky Party Game

The Hair Salon: Lesbian Voyeur Erotica

Tribadism 1: Girls Only Sex Workshop

Tribadism 2: The Art of Scissoring

Tribadism 3: Threeway Hookups

The Kiss: A Game of Oral Sex

Pledge Week: Sorority Sisters

Carny Games 1: A Wild Sex Party

Carny Games 2: A Kinky Sex Party

Carny Games 3: An Erotic Sex Party

Dreamscape: An Artificial Reality Game

Glory Hole: Guess Who's On the Other Side

Joy Ride: A Late Night Erotic Bus Trip

The Blind Girl: An Erotic Romance(Coming Soon)

Lesbian Erotica Bundles:

Jade's Erotic Adventures: Books 1 - 5

Jade's Erotic Adventures: Books 6 - 10

Jade's Erotic Adventures: Books 11 - 15

Jade's Erotic Adventures: Books 16 - 20

Jade's Erotic Adventures: Books 21 - 25

Jade's Erotic Adventures: Books 26 - 30

Jade's Erotic Adventures: Books 31 - 35

Jade's Erotic Adventures: Books 36 - 40

Jade's Erotic Adventures: Books 41 - 45

Jade's Erotic Adventures: Books 46 - 50

Fifty Shades of Jade: Superbundle

Standalone Stories:

The Polynesian Girl: A Lesbian EroticRomance

FOLLOW VICTORIA RUSH:

Want to keep informed of my latest erotic book releases? Sign up for my newsletter and receive a FREE bonus book:

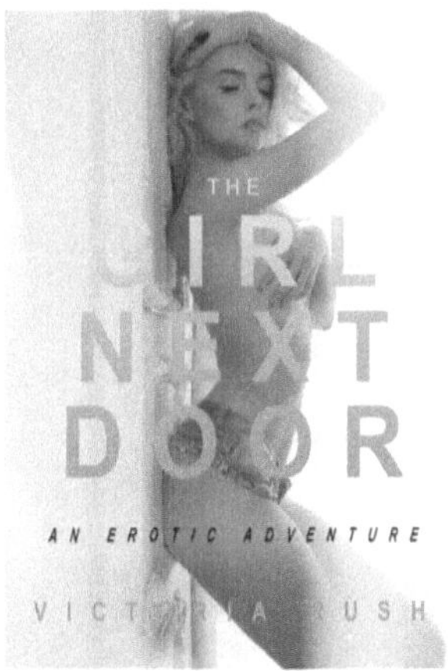

Spying on the neighbors just got a lot more interesting...